MURDER *by* NUMBERS

A SHELL ISLE MYSTERY

Tonya Penrose

This is a work of fiction. Names, characters, places, and incidents are products of the author's imagination or are used fictitiously and are not to be construed as real. Any resemblance to actual events, locations, organizations, or persons, living or dead, is entirely coincidental.

World Castle Publishing, LLC
Pensacola, Florida
Copyright © 2025 Tonya Penrose
Hardback ISBN: 9798291104972
Paperback ISBN: 9798891264366
eBook ISBN: 9798891264373
Second Edition, World Castle Publishing, LLC, August 25, 2025
http://www.worldcastlepublishing.com
Licensing Notes
Cover: Cover Designs by Karen

This book is dedicated to all the curious ones out there.
Surprises always await you.

CHAPTER 1

A smile dressed Page's face as she held The Perk Coffee Shop's door open for her cousin, Betsy. "What's got you all sappy, happy, and crooning some unrecognizable tune?"

Betsy spun around. "Well, for starters, I feel sappy happy because we've made it through the rest of the summer without you snagging another murder mystery for us to solve. Plus, we've been able to focus on growing our new business venture at Honey Bees. My life has actually felt normal the last couple of months, not chasing after baddies. And don't you do anything to change it." Betsy tugged the brightly-flowered Mumu over her generous hips and, with a wink, sauntered inside.

Page followed her to the coffee bar. "Duly noted, Bets, but when I get an inkling, you know —"

"For once, ignore any more of those trouble-making inklings. We're all about living the good life at Shell Isle with plenty of beach time." Betsy's flushed face complemented her auburn wavy hair. Once upon a time, called willowy, her figure now testified to her enjoyment of their Honey Bees Shop's many baked delectables.

"Is there more to this sharing?" Page tucked her sunglasses into her handbag.

"Of course. I'm a cornucopia of words. Nice image for

the harvest season, huh?" Betsy did a mock preening.

"The best. No finer. Pray continue. The barista is waiting for our order. I fear we'll be standing here until the cows come home."

"What does that mean?" Betsy cocked an eyebrow. "Oh, funny. You're being sarcastic, referring to having to wait. Continuing, fall is in the air, which means it's time for Honey Bees to embrace baking everything pumpkin. Yes, ma'am, envision pumpkin donuts, pumpkin cookies, pumpkin cupcakes, pumpkin—"

Amusement found Page's eyes as she reached for Betsy's arm. "Stifle your pumpkin-loving self. Honey Bees is more than a bakery. You're ignoring that we've added all the lovely honey body products to our inventory. Honestly, your world revolves around sweets. Besides, not everyone likes pumpkin."

Betsy pulled a face and turned to the barista. "I want a large frozen pumpkin latte with extra whipped cream. Make that two. I'm treating Ms. Pumpkin Humbug."

"No whipped cream on mine. And I am not a humbug." Page scrunched her freckled nose at Betsy and moved her petite frame toward their two favorite wing-back chairs tucked in the corner. The Perk had an interesting vibe with its eclectic décor that suited their patrons' tastes. Page glanced around the coffee shop. Shell Isle's quilters sat exclaiming over colorful squares of material displayed on the antique oak table. A young couple cuddled on a brocade loveseat, whispering and smiling into each other's eyes.

Page noted a somewhat familiar-faced middle-aged

man sitting alone at a nearby table. She couldn't place him, but they'd interacted before, maybe at Honey Bees. Something in the classified section of the newspaper kept his pen moving and his mouth mumbling. She watched as his bushy brows created a furrow deeper than the Grand Canyon. A wise-guy type with a sinister glare joined him. Page guessed the navy parka on an eighty-degree day probably meant he was carrying. He exuded a 'bust your chops' kind of air. Page felt uneasy when his beady, dark eyes darted around The Perk and landed on her. She grabbed a magazine and pretended interest in a story. Hearing muffled, heated words flying back and forth across the table, Page stole a peek.

The wise guy stood and did something Page found peculiar. With an abrupt exchange of laptops, the wise guy stormed past Page toward the exit. Within seconds, a new inkling came with the realization that more than coffee was brewing at The Perk. Betsy's approach interrupted her further eavesdropping.

"Here you go. One pumpkin latte sans cream. Ya know, the joint looks pretty empty this morning." Betsy's eyes took in the few people seated nearby.

"Thanks for the coffee. Yep, guess Monday's off to a quiet start." Page's gaze returned to the man now scanning the newspaper again. His pen went to work marking the classified ads. *Maybe he's job-hunting,* surmised Page. Her cousin's voice cut off more musings. As for the inkling, she'd ignore it...for the moment.

Betsy released a heavy sigh. "Geez. Get a load of the young love over on that sofa. I hate having to watch smooching when you've sentenced me to this long exile from men."

Page sucked in a breath. "As I've explained a gazillion times, I think you'd benefit from not getting into other male relationships until your choosing improves." With a chuckle, Page turned to her cousin. "Betsy Ross, face it; you pick lousy, and worst of all, you marry most of them."

Betsy pulled her hand fan from her flowered tote. "Why did I have to bring up men and activate my hot flashes? Okay, I grant you I'm a disaster at picking men, but I can bake like nobody's—who are you watching?" Betsy twisted in her seat to look.

"Shh. Not so loud. See that middle-aged, slouchy-dressed guy a few feet away with the bushy eyebrows and bald head? He just had a run-in with a man whose name should be Knuckles. They exchanged laptops, which I think appeared rather odd."

"I don't see anyone—"

"Look to your left. The one who just mopped his forehead with a handkerchief." Page took a sip of her latte.

"Oh, him. That's Mister No Personality. I can't remember his name, but I heard he's from the northeast. He's the new high school math teacher and not too well-liked according to my sources." Betsy waved her hand. "Aren't I impressive, having the skinny?"

Page bobbed her head, causing her honey-colored topknot to droop. Annoyed, she clipped it higher. She filed away Betsy's scoop. "What else do you know about him?"

Betsy tapped her chin and looked up at the ceiling. "He's single. That's all I can recall. Anyway, I like to keep up on Shell Isle doings." Betsy's focus returned to the mound of whipped cream, threatening to slide down her cup. She took a read on Page. "Don't start. He's not my type."

Glancing back at the teacher, a smile quivered on Page's mouth. "No, he's definitely not for you. We know him, right?" She slipped a napkin to Betsy. The drips had found her Mumu.

"We do. He's a regular customer every Wednesday morning, ordering a fresh popover. Word's on the street that our Ina's popovers are sublime. You know we sold out in an hour last week? Wait. You weren't there. That was the day you and Detective Dreamboat went sailing."

"Would you please and thank you stop calling Steve my Detective Dreamboat? We enjoy each other's company, love to sail, and he lives next door. It's all easy. Plus, need I remind you that we should stay on Steve's good side? His help proved invaluable with our last two murder-solving escapades. Besides, I've told you, I'm not getting serious with any man. Light romance, I can do. My lifestyle as a single woman suits me just fine." Page released a huff.

"So, you say. Need I remind you Dreamboat refers to us at the police station as the Shell Isle Snoops? Most unflattering, and after we pretty much solved their last two murder investigations. You might want to take that up with him next time you're lollygagging on his sailboat." Betsy batted her eyes.

Page swatted the air. "Oh, I don't pay any attention to that nonsense. We're talented sleuths. Those detectives are slow learners, but they need us. Grief, but that guy perspires nonstop. He's back to wiping his face. What's that about?" Page frowned.

Betsy sneaked a look. "I didn't know men suffered from hot flashes? Did you? There must be a female god, after all, who divvies up hormonal things fairly. I love it."

Page laughed. "I don't think men get flashes, but I do think this man—has an affliction with the classified section. Something's up with him." Page watched as the flustered math teacher disconnected from a cell phone call and hurried out of The Perk, mumbling. "Listen, Bets, you need to hear what I witnessed a few minutes ago—"

"No, no, no witnessing. We're not starting the first day of fall getting tangled up with—where are you going?" Betsy tried and failed to grab Page's arm.

"Sit tight. Back in a sec." Page snagged the section of the newspaper he'd left behind.

"Why are you toting that coffee-stained paper over to our table? Yuck." Betsy scooted back into her chair, adding distance.

Ignoring her cousin, Page studied the circled numbers. "Curious, so very curious."

"Don't say curious. I hate it when you say that word. It always means that my life is about to—"

"Look at this, Betsy. I wonder what's so special about these random numbers that Slouch marked? And listen to what the ad he starred says."

Betsy leaned forward. "No. I don't want to listen to you read some dumb ad and try to make something of it. Give me that paper. Forget Slouch as you've now dubbed him."

Betsy's hand reached out, but Page was faster.

"Would you listen, please? It says: 'The next cipher clock ticks at 2100, September 22. Numbers posted.' That doesn't sound good to me." Page sighed and looked over at her cousin.

"Of course, it doesn't sound good. You're bored and looking for another mystery." Jamming the straw to the bottom of her cup, Betsy took a gulp. "Please forget this and toss the paper. Come on. Let's get to Honey Bees."

Page's eyes returned to the random numbers circled on different ads. "These have to mean something along with that ad's message. And don't forget the encounter with Knuckles. It means—"

Betsy stood. "It means something to Slouch, but not to us. I repeat, not to us."

"I fear it will soon," Page said under her breath and followed Betsy outside.

CHAPTER 2

Time quickly devoured the cousins' afternoon at Honey Bees. Ina and Betsy kept a steady stream of pumpkin-frosted cookies and cupcakes emerging from the back kitchen. Page watched as Daisy, a recent addition to the shop staff, faced the easel and drew baked goods illustrations next to the announcement of Pumpkin Delectables.

"You like?" Daisy's smile mirrored her sunny disposition and name. Jeans and a printed yellow tee showing bumble bees pollinating flowers had become her work uniform. The young woman's plaited cornsilk hair and a dab of coral lip gloss completed the casual image. "I love creating these drawings on the board."

"You get my token gold star, Miss Daisy," answered Page. "Thanks for another productive day. Ina's already left, so why don't you take off? Betsy and I will close up."

"Okay, thanks." Daisy grabbed her backpack. "Tomorrow morning, I'll place the sign outside on the sidewalk to attract any passersby." With a wave, she disappeared out the door.

Page gave herself kudos for making Daisy a full-time employee. The recent college graduate had proven her value by generating impressive marketing ideas to grow Honey Bees' bottom line. Detective Koch had every reason to be proud of his daughter. Page felt pleased to have the opportunity to mentor the young woman in the best practices of starting a new business.

Having Ina in charge of baking relieved Page from worrying about Betsy's propensity to create culinary debacles. Her cousin felt spice belonged in and on every morsel that entered a mouth. Fiery hot was Betsy's trademark, as proven by the large bottle of antacids in Page's handbag.

Page acknowledged three facts that kept her life at Shell Isle from being perfect. Betsy's ongoing presence in the cottage's guest room. Her cousin had become a fixture since Page inherited Hibiscus from their Aunt Tilly. Second, Betsy's bungalow renovation seemingly had no end. Third, Bets had commandeered the kitchen only to produce awful, unholy meals for them. Her cousin viewed the cooking contribution as payback for the gratuitous lodging. Page, however, thought it qualified as her personal karmic payback from a past life transgression.

With a heavy sigh, Page reflected on overhearing an earlier telephone conversation with Betsy and her contractor. Every time the guy seemed close to wrapping the job, Betsy came up with another idea to improve the bungalow. Page had lost count of how many paint colors had been dismissed once on the walls. Her persnickety cousin claimed the natural light in coastal Carolina kept changing the ambiance of the shade. Peach melba was Bet's latest selection. Of course, it would be a shade named after a dessert.

"There you are. No doubt lost in some notion about Detective Dreamboat." Betsy batted her eyelashes. "No, don't bother answering. I've got a simply swell dinner idea. We stop by the store so I can grab a nice leg of lamb for me to prepare. I've imagined the ideal spice rub dancing in my head with loads of colorful peppercorns — "

"Actually, I've got a proposal as well. I think you'll take to it." Panic washed over Page as she scrambled to come up with something to avoid a leg of lamb becoming a fire starter in her oven.

"I'm listening. Make it good." Betsy emptied the cash register and tucked the money bag into her handbag for a bank deposit.

Mickey entered the shop, buying Page more time. "Hiya gals. I'm dropping off the honey order." He parked the cardboard box on the counter.

"Super, Mickey. Hey, we missed seeing you at The Perk earlier." Page peeked inside the box.

"Yep. I've got the day off. Even the bowling alley cut me loose tonight." Mickey grinned. "I'm what you call a free agent."

"Well, I'm glad the Mermaids aren't bowling tonight. You're my lucky charm." Betsy patted Mickey's arm.

"Wow! You scored gold. Look, Bets!" Page held up a small jar of cognac-colored honey.

"Is that — ?"

"Yep, your special Tibetan honey. The elixir of the gods. Remember to use it sparingly and with care." Mickey's expression grew somber.

"Don't fret. We're mindful of its unique gift." Page nodded.

The entrance bell jingled, causing three faces to turn.

Page watched Detective Steve Tanner enter wearing his dashingly handsome grin. Jeans and a black polo shirt were his standard detective attire, along with the police shield clipped to his leather belt. She could see the outline of the gun tucked in his pocket. Page appreciated that he made a point of blending into the casual Shell Isle lifestyle.

"Afternoon, snoops. Hiya, Mick." Steve approached the group.

Betsy pulled her shoulders back. "Would you please stop calling us snoops? The correct word is sleuths, mister."

"I call 'em like I see 'em." Steve snagged the last cookie on a tray. "Ina's?" he asked before biting into it.

Page smiled, knowing if Betsy's baking hand had been on the cookie, he'd put it back. "Yes, sir, Ina's freshly-baked pumpkin cream walnut cookie." Page finished unpacking the jars of flavored honey.

"But it's my recipe," interjected Betsy.

"Guess I'll risk it." Steve popped the cookie in his mouth. "Hey, this is really good. Got more?"

Page handed him a napkin. "No. You ate the last of the harvest cookies. So, what brought you in to see us? Perhaps you need help with a case?"

Mickey snickered. Seeing both women send him a glare, he looked at the floor and grew quiet.

"Actually, I stopped by to invite you both to Movie on the Green tonight. Thought we'd grab some submarine sandwiches to bring along. Interested?" Steve moved closer to Page and tucked his arm around her waist.

"Depends. What's playing?" asked Betsy. She flicked off the lights.

"Your favorite genre…a mystery called *The Willow Inn Murders*. So, what do you say?" A smile curled on Steve's mouth.

"I say, may I come along? I've become quite fond of detective flicks since cozying up with these two snoops… sleuths." Mickey's eyes sparkled.

"The more, the merrier. Ladies?" Steve glanced down at Page.

Page caught Betsy's nod. "We're in. Sounds like fun." She tried to ignore the dimples that melted her every time. Since meeting her neighbor, Steve Tanner, the traitorous hormones had become a real annoyance. She'd been trying and failing to ignore her attraction to him. Page forced her thoughts back to the invitation. "What time?"

"Why don't you two walk over to my bungalow around seven o'clock. I'll have four roast beef subs packed in the cooler. Mickey, we'll meet you at the park. Listen, I need to dash. I've got a lead to track down. See you later." Steve winked at Page and hurried out the door.

"I need to skedaddle too. Count on me to bring drinks. Thanks for letting me tag along." Mickey grabbed the now-empty cardboard box.

"We'll see you later. Come on, Page. I want to hurry to the cottage and make homemade jalapeño honey mustard potato chips for tonight. Maybe with a dash of marjoram and something else I'm keeping to myself." Betsy smacked her lips.

"Those chips sound...never mind, I'm ready. Got the key in the door." Page waved Mickey off and hunted for a peppermint to settle her tummy. Just hearing what Betsy was adding to the picnic menu woke up her taxed digestive system.

Page's mind flashed on the earlier inkling and sighed. She sensed outside forces were conspiring to do harm, which meant one thing. Her sleuthing gift would soon get tapped.

CHAPTER 3

"Would you please hurry? I see Detective Dreamboat leaning against the SUV, and he looks impatient." Betsy turned from the window and draped the large, flowered tote over her shoulder.

Page appeared wearing jeans and a red-checked cotton shirt. Gold hoop earrings and a muted red lipstick completed her look. "Sorry, I had to grab two blankets for us. Let's go."

Betsy burst into laughter. "You do know you're wearing a tablecloth that screams I'm a picnic."

"I was trying to reflect our outing theme. Too much?" Page glanced at her shirt.

Betsy's laugh grew louder.

"Hush already. Back in a flash." Page hurried down the hall and into her bedroom, muttering, "I do not look like a tablecloth." She slipped on a boring black t-shirt and returned to find Betsy outside.

Page approached her waiting friends. "Here I am with the blankets. I'm starving." She climbed into the passenger side.

Steve took the blankets to stow in the back. "Where's the red picnic tablecloth? Betsy said you were—"

Page glared at Betsy. "My cousin has a warped sense of humor, and she's a blabbermouth. Can we please go?"

Betsy scrunched down in the backseat. "I fear payback is in my immediate future."

The blankets were laid out within twenty minutes, and the food was released from the bags and Betsy's tote. Mickey appeared with the cooler of sodas and joined the seated bunch. Music played through the speakers until the movie screen came to life.

The residents of Shell Isle turned out whenever a fun event made the calendar. Tonight was no exception. Kids ran around waving neon light sticks purchased from a nearby vendor. At the same time, parents attempted to corral them to eat before the movie began. Page noticed a cart with a sign promising ice cream. No doubt, Betsy would zero in on that soon enough and cause trouble for Page's waistline. The second inkling came unexpectedly. Something was imminent, signaling Page to remain alert.

"Here you go, everyone. My homemade Hotsy Totsy Chips, which I must warn you, are spectacular." Betsy passed a plastic bag toward the guys. "Dig in. Plenty for all."

Steve's eyebrow went up, showing his concern. "Uhm, thanks, Betsy." He put two on his plate and made eye contact with Page.

A brave Mickey grabbed a handful and plopped one in his mouth. Within seconds, coughing commenced. Tears ran down his cheeks. "Damn, if these things aren't a touch fiery. Think I need me a chaser from that cooler."

An amused Steve tossed a cola Mickey's way. "I appreciate you being the Guinea pig tonight."

"Guinea pig? Should I feel offended?" Betsy paused

and studied the three faces. "My chips are savory with a kiss of heat to awaken any stray dormant taste buds. That's the secret to my culinary genius. Right Page?"

"So much hot genius, Betsy," Page managed to get the words out with a straight face while watching Mickey guzzle the soda's contents without a pause. She noticed Steve's two chips remained untouched. He wasn't out of the woods.

Betsy pointed at Steve's paper plate. She grabbed a handful of her savory offering and deposited them. "There you go. Don't be so shy. Plenty for all."

Steve nodded. "Mickey, toss me a drink, will ya?" He bit off a tiny piece of a chip and dashed the heat with the cold drink. "Say, Betsy, what else you got for us in the tote?" When Betsy looked away, Steve buried the chips under the corner of the blanket and grinned at Page.

"Let's see. I baked cookies." Betsy pulled out a plastic container. "You have to wait until intermission for these melt-in-your-mouthers."

"It's going to be hard, but we'll sure try," said Mickey, finally able to talk.

The rest of their picnic was uneventful as the group exchanged news and gossip moving around the town. Further chatter ceased when the park's pole lights dimmed, and the movie screen came to life. Page felt Steve take her hand. At fifty-something, attraction still held her captive to male charms.

~*~

"What an enjoyable mystery. It's intermission, so we can chat about whodunit. Here we go. Cookies for one and all." Betsy held the container in the air. Her damp curls had morphed into frizz balls from the humidity.

"You all start without me. I'm heading over to the ice cream cart. I'm craving a banana popsicle." Page stood.

"But my cookies —"

"Oh, I plan to eat at least two of them when I get back," Page assured her cousin and hoped she could deliver. Thankfully, no one asked to accompany her. She needed to follow the inkling alone.

Page felt the push to take the long way around to the ice cream vendor. The park's small office building was attached to a large open-air pavilion. Approaching, she noticed a few people gathered around a wooden picnic table. An argument had ensued with voices sounding hotter than Betsy's chips. Page moved closer and found a lush hibiscus bush to tuck behind. The breeze brought their exchange to her ears.

A man's voice spoke, "I'm telling you three that I want out of this racket. You've gone too far infiltrating. These people play for keeps, and we're going to all end up at the bottom of Shell Bay with cement shoes."

Page watched a dark-haired woman in her fifties turn to face the man who'd just spoken. His back was to Page, so she couldn't make out his features.

"Dean, you fool, there's no getting out. You know too much. Taking over the number-running cipher sealed your fate. If you're as smart as you led everyone to think, you'll shut your mouth now and hope one of us doesn't see you as a problem to remedy. Are you getting my drift?" An icicle was warmer than the woman's tone.

"Ease up, Jewel. Our pal here knows the score," said a second man. His laugh sounded anything but friendly to Page. His stocky shape looked like it could deliver pain, but not feel much.

Jewel sat back. "I'm not convinced of that, Lucky, far from it. We're going to need some proof from Dean that his loyalty is ironclad. Don't you agree, Stella?"

Page watched as the flashy blonde rubbed Dean's neck. "Right, Jewel. My big boy is a player. He just got off track for a moment. Didn't you, hun? Tell Jewel that you're ready for the eleven o'clock exchange."

"Yeah, I'm prepared, and I figured out the formula's code. Forget what I said. It won't happen again. I got rattled earlier by something that happened unrelated to our work. Sorry, Jewel. Sorry, Lucky." He twisted on the bench seat.

Page gulped when she saw the man's face. It was the math teacher from The Perk involved with this motley bunch. Knuckles flashed in her mind. He was absent from the soiree.

Seeing no one around, Jewel continued, "I've got another code coming in and it must be worked quickly. It's the most critical piece we've been given. A lot of money and power rides on solving it." Her voice had a savage edge to it.

"What, what kind of code is it?" Dean stammered out. "I'm not good at complicated ciphers requiring—"

Jewel leaned forward. "Hear me, Dean. After your little episode tonight, you'd better not mess this up."

Lucky reached across the table and yanked Dean's collar forward. "Didn't you hear our Jewel? It ain't optional. You cipher or else."

Dean coughed when Lucky released the shirt. "Sure, sure. I can do it. Just tell me what you need."

"Take this envelope." Jewel shoved it across the table. "The instructions are inside. Watch the classifieds starting tomorrow for the rest of what you need to know. Same procedure as the other times. Got it?"

"You got it. Don't ya, baby?" Stella touched Dean's cheek and then gave it a pinch that meant business.

Dean pulled out his handkerchief and wiped his forehead. "Yes, I understand. I'll make sure tonight's handoff happens, and I'll drop your money at the same place."

Page could tell Dean was a mess and in a mess. Seeing them ready to leave, she backed silently away. The earlier inklings had led her to this place. Glancing at the moon, she watched a grey cloud extinguish the moonlight. An all-too-familiar foreboding washed over Page.

The ice cream cart waited ahead, but Page's taste for a banana popsicle was gone. Still, she couldn't return to the bunch without something. Plastering a smile on her face, Page reentered her ordinary world.

CHAPTER 4

"Here you go. Popsicles for everyone." Page smiled and waved them in the air. "I've got cherry, grape, and orange." She laid them on top of the cooler. "You can fight over who gets what. I've got my banana." Page unwrapped hers and plopped down next to Steve. "So good."

Steve cut a grin. "I can tell you're into it. Ah, to be a banana—"

"I want none of that hanky-panky talk around me. I'm still living the life of a romance shut-in." Betsy claimed the orange popsicle. "This cold should help my flash."

"I've got nothing to say about any of that. Page, hand me the cherry flavor." Mickey chuckled and put out his hand.

"You got it, Mickey, and the grape goes to our favorite detective." Page caught sight of Dean walking past with his head drooped, and shoulders slumped to the ground.

Steve followed Page's gaze. "There's a guy dragging the anchor. Know him?"

Betsy gave a glance. "Oh, that's Mr. No Personality. Page has dubbed him 'slouch.' He's the new math teacher."

"I hear he's not too popular at the high school," added Mickey.

Page noticed everyone's lips were the color of their popsicles. She elected to keep silent and enjoy the colorful talk. "I saw him at The Perk earlier today. He had a thing going with—"

"Don't say another word, Page Wright, or I swear I'll channel Aunt Tilly down to mess with you," Betsy threatened. She turned to Steve, "Page is trying to make something out of nothing. We're changing the subject. Who wants a cookie? I haven't had any takers yet."

"Fine. I will keep my observations to myself. What's in the cookies?" Page reached for the container and took a sniff. "Here you go, Mickey. Be a good sport again."

Steve laughed and looked away when Betsy glared.

"It's a new recipe. Oatmeal raisin with a twist." Betsy handed out napkins.

"I'm gonna need to be knowin' what kinda twist," said Mickey, accepting only one cookie from Page. She knew he'd wised up after the firecracker potato chips.

Page deposited four on Steve's napkin with a wicked grin. "For the guy with a big appetite. Come on, Bets, tell us the secret sauce here."

"I added cayenne, of course, for zing. A splash of rum and a few black beans for moisture and ginseng for friskiness," Betsy whispered. She took an impressive bite. "Could use a smidge more cayenne pepper."

Page snagged three of Steve's cookies and put them back in the container.

"Ginseng got you worried, Sherlocka?" Steve asked, amusement dressing his face.

"Ignore their hormone imbalances. What do you think, Mickey?" asked Betsy.

Forced to eat the offering, Mickey moved his soda closer and broke off a chunk. Silence reigned supreme while he chewed. "Think you got the pepper about right. The beans sure add — "

"Texture?" offered Betsy.

"Yep. Texture. Filling things." Mickey snagged another napkin.

Page knew that trick. She'd been using it for months. The contents deposited and disposed of in that saving square of paper were her saving grace at most Betsy meals.

Intermission ended, darkness descended, and the cookies disappeared. Page kept fretting over Dean. She felt sure he'd gotten involved in shady doings at Shell Isle. The beauty of the beach town seemed like a magnet for all types. What newcomers soon discovered was the community's vibe shunned most who didn't have a long-term connection there. Everyone knew the police department had zero tolerance for any shenanigans.

With Steve's background as a past Navy Seal and strong FBI affiliation, the part-time detective had proved a deterrent to any local petty criminals. Any new arrivals who attempted to set up an illegal shop at Shell soon met with the wrath of Detectives Koch and Tanner.

Page's thoughts shifted to recalling how Steve Tanner's dog, Barnacle, had brought them together with his many uninvited visits to her cottage. Having a detective next door gave Page extra security and helpful information when an inkling presented a case. Steve had required some convincing and proving before he recognized the value of her intuitive gift. Still, he was quick to chastise when she flirted with anything remotely concerning. They'd carved out what Page felt was the ideal arrangement. A mutual respect in crime-solving, a solid friendship, and a budding romance.

"Hey, Page, do you think the son killed his grandfather?" Betsy brought Page back to the present. "He looks mighty suspicious to me."

Page's mind scrambled for an answer. She hadn't a clue what was happening in the movie. "Uhm, that's a good guess, Bets."

"Really? I figured you'd zero in on the aunt. She's got plenty of motivation." Steve winked at Betsy.

"Oh, her, yes." Page glanced at the screen, seeing an interrogation scene. "The aunt is a strong possibility."

Steve chuckled. "Sherlocka, you're so busted. There's no aunt." He touched her chin and moved it toward the screen. "Stop thinking about the math teacher. Your sleuthing skills are needed for this flick."

"Yep, he's got ya, Page," Mickey added.

"You all don't play fair." Page repositioned herself on the blanket. "No more talk. I've gotta catch up with the story, so I can solve this whodunit for you slow types."

~*~

Back at Hibiscus, the cousins ventured onto the screened porch. Betsy claimed the hammock while Page settled in the glider. Ten o'clock still felt early enough for them to entertain more activity. Beach goers hung around until midnight, enjoying a more relaxed time. Sand buckets were replaced by small nets to capture what the tide brought for inspection.

Page noticed the breeze had moved elsewhere, leaving the ocean eerily calm. She watched a family with flashlights searching the tidal pools for crabs. A teenage boy and girl had parked themselves in the lifeguard's abandoned chair for a night of cuddling. Even the moon had found a place to hide from the clouds and illuminated the beach in a bluish light. Everything appeared normal, but Page suspected that the illusion would soon be broken. Another inkling hit, and this time, she knew the destination. "Hey, Bets, how about a bike ride up to the pier and marina? We've got time to get some exercise before bedtime."

Betsy stretched and closed her latest historical romance novel. "Hmm. I suppose I could use a bit of pedaling after I sampled Ina's pumpkin donuts the whole day. Besides, Dowager Margaret is a big bore. I miss the Dowager Gertrude. Now there was a woman who knew how to interact with the Ton. She could —"

Page pulled Betsy out of the hammock. "Never mind your issue with the latest dowager. I'll get the bikes from the shed, and you grab us a couple of waters and our cell phones. Hup two."

"Okay, okay. I'm hupping, whatever that means." Betsy headed to the kitchen.

Page wiped the bikes down with a towel and leaned them against the walkway's wood railing. The cottage's beach access was only a few steps down. Page stole a glance at Steve's bungalow and saw his yellow surfboard resting on the picnic table. At least she didn't have to worry about the distraction of him looking all sexy riding a wave to perfection. She'd need Betsy's hot flash fan if her mind continued down this road.

"Here's your phone and water. Where's the breeze?" Betsy maneuvered her bicycle onto the sand.

"No breeze. You'll make your own soon enough by pedaling." Page followed close behind. "Let's take the bikes further out to the hard sand. We've got plenty, since it's low tide."

The two cousins rode in silence, each finding needed solitude. The sounds of the bicycle's tires squishing the sand became hypnotic. Salt cloaked the air in a warm blanket. Peace descended on the two riders.

Page saw the fishing poles lined up like sentinels along the pier's railing. Devoted and determined fishers weren't letting the late hour send them home. Shell Isle enjoyed the blessing of abundant fish and shellfish in its waters thanks to careful monitoring and limits placed on catches. Page had learned the rules after their last murder investigation. She and Betsy had played a pivotal role in nabbing some real low-life selling illegal shark fins.

Parking their bikes in the rack, Page watched her cousin guzzle her bottle of water. "You realize you don't have any liquid for the ride back."

Betsy wiped the damp curls from her forehead. "Oh, I'll have a beverage. Don't you worry. The bait shop is open until midnight, and Harold's got my favorite brand of root beer all chilled and waiting."

"Silly me. I should have known you'd have drinks and

such mapped out in advance. Want to stroll out to the pier and see what's happening?" Page gazed at where the boats were moored in a protected area of the small marina. Steve's sailboat, Carpe Diem, looked lonely. Maybe he'd ask her to go sailing the coming weekend. She turned to Betsy. "Lead the way. I brought money for our pier entrance."

"Excellent. And I've got the jingle for the root beers. Let's get to the fishing action. I love it when they bring in a shark, even though they have to toss it back."

Page shook her head. "You're warped, Betsy Ross. Really warped, but I love you just the same." The nudge came to walk over to the marina dock. *Not yet, please. Give me a few minutes to mentally prepare*, Page mumbled to herself. She peeked at her watch. The timing fit the inkling, the ad, and what she'd overheard with Dean's group.

CHAPTER 5

"Well, wasn't that pier expedition a big bust? Not a single shark was brought in. Not even the usual shark feeding frenzy when the fishermen dump fish guts off the side." Betsy released a humph for added drama.

"I hear your disappointment. The nerve of those sharks not to show up for your entertainment tonight. We must voice this complaint to Harold. Let's grab our sodas." Page eyed the marina and got the nudge. Now, she was needed.

"You're mocking me. I can always tell. You're missing the fine points about how fascinating sharks are. For instance, did you know sharks don't have bones?" Betsy entered the bait shop.

"Of course, they have bones. Where did you learn this?" Page opened the beverage cooler door and snagged two cans.

"I went to the University of Betsy Knows All." Betsy sashayed to the counter. "Hiya, Harold. No sharks around tonight. You should refund us our pier walk money."

Harold rubbed his chin. "Ah, Betsy, you know I can't give refunds for that reason. How about I let you in free next time?"

Page smiled reassuringly at Harold and passed the drink money. "Ignore her. She's grumpy without sugar every thirty seconds."

"I am not grumpy. My expectations were not met," replied Betsy, tilting her chin upward.

"Bye, Harold. Come on, expert on all things 'shark.' Walk with me to the marina. Steve told me he put some new colorful telltales on Carpe's sails."

"What do I care about tall tales? Let's head back to Hibiscus. I want my bed." Betsy sipped her drink and followed Page.

"It's telltales. Tall tales are what you spin about Steve and me." Page laughed and looped her arm through Betsy's. For the moment, she'd avoid awakening Betsy's suspicions.

"Don't get me wound up about you and Dreamboat pretending there isn't some heavy kissing and who knows what else happening under my nose. Betsy Ross, the possible ancestor to the sewer of our flag, is no fool when it comes to romantic antics."

"Ha. You might want to retract that statement." Page kept them moving toward the marina. "Let me help you. In the past couple of years, we had Fred, who had something to do with poultry. William designed some app to identify rodent mitigation. Then my personal favorite was Jasper from Mississippi, and I still can't figure the attraction there. And Alton with his oodles of generational money. I don't think I left anyone of consequence out."

"Hold up right there." Betsy put one hand on her hip. "For your information, Fred's family owns one of the largest poultry processing plants in our country. There was a problem I couldn't get past. Alas, the man kept showing up for dates with feathers in his toupee. William's app was a major help to cities with a rat infestation. Still, I couldn't get him to talk about anything other than rat reproduction and mitigation techniques."

"Please. Must you continue?" teased Page.

"Yes. I must continue to defend my reputation you've besmirched." Betsy held her head high.

"Go ahead," Page said, her face bemused.

"So, you know my devout affection toward natural fibers. You didn't know, but Jasper owns a string of cotton gins." Betsy paused. "Get it? String? Cotton?"

"Oh, yes, very witty. Are we done here?" asked Page.

"No," snapped Betsy. "Jasper liked that I appreciated cotton's many attributes. We were hitting it off quite well. Unfortunately, there was a little episode involving me and his false teeth. We will not speak further on this…ever."

"Darn. That story sounds like something I could have sunk my teeth into. Get it? Teeth—" Page jumped back, missing Betsy's attempt at smacking her arm.

"Would you please let me finish my tale of love woe? Yes, Alton had moola, but he spent too much time napping, and he drooled. I'm overdue for a man who arrives in my life without some—"

"Keep walking. That's the most pathetic run-down of your love life I've heard to date. And, cousin, I've listened to decades of your romantic escapades. This accounting may well get you an early release from the no-dating moratorium." Page nodded, keeping her amusement inside. Betsy was colorful in every aspect of how she lived life.

"Why in all that's holy didn't I tell you of my trials and tribulations sooner? You've just changed my whole grumpy self into a happy self. Now, I'm willing to follow you—" Betsy halted. Her expression changed to puzzlement.

"Isn't that the math teacher sitting sort of funny on the bench? Look to your right near the charter fishing boats?" Betsy pointed out.

In an instant, Page knew the inkling had delivered. She stood next to Betsy, taking in the scene. "It does look like him. Let's just amble by and see what he's doing. Remember the ad I read to you at The Perk? It said the cipher clock starts ticking at eleven o'clock. When I left you all for the popsicles tonight, I overheard that he had some rendezvous set for eleven tonight. It all ties together."

"So what if it does? We're not getting involved in this guy's business. No ambling." Betsy started to turn back.

"Hang on a sec. I'm going to sit by him on the bench and see what I can find out." Page tapped Betsy's shoulder to get her attention. "I got a nudge a few minutes ago. We're about to get involved in something."

"Seriously? Again? I may have a hissy fit right here. I may enjoy a big cry. I may even stomp my sore left foot. Why, you ask?"

Page couldn't help the escaping smile. She knew where Betsy was heading. "Tell me."

"I was *this* close." Betsy spaced two fingers an inch apart. "*This* close to having a 'get out of man-jail card' to act on. Within a minute, I find my fate is sucking me into some dirty doings by a math teacher, which, incidentally, I could give two flips about tonight."

"Done hissying?" asked Page.

"Probably not." Betsy tossed her soda can into the receptacle and scrutinized the teacher. "Okay, I'll wait here while you go cozy up to Mister No Personality. Be quick, or I may not have the energy to pedal my sad sack home."

"Thanks, Bets. Back in a flash." Page walked the distance to where Dean sat and joined him. The closest dock light was burned out, so they sat in darkness. She stared at the boats tied down before speaking. "I love the sound of the sailboats talking amongst themselves."

Silence came from Dean.

Well, he's quit mumbling, so that's a good sign. Page tried again. "It's like they're exchanging stories of their last outing or something like that. Do you sail?"

Dean offered no answer.

Page felt the nudge signaling her to act. She bent forward to get a closer look. Dean appeared to be asleep. She motioned for Betsy to join her.

"What? Do you want to introduce us? Hi, I'm Betsy Ross, and no jokes about my name." Betsy put her hand out and got nothing in return. "He's passed out. Just great. Now, we have to get him help."

"Yeah, we're going to need help, but not for him. I fear the worst, Betsy."

"No, you don't. He's just drunk. I think I can smell the booze. Probably rum." Betsy touched his shoulder. "Hey, Dean. Rise and shine." He fell sideways on the bench.

"Heads or tails." Page tossed the coin, refusing to let

her emotions gain control.

"Tails." Betsy stepped back and sucked in a breath.

"Tails it is. I lose." Page punched in the numbers on her cell phone. "Steve, we need you at the marina. Yes, I know what time it is. Yes, we're fine, but someone else isn't." Page disconnected and saw two familiar faces stepping into a boat. Within seconds, the engine throttled forward, and the boat pulled away, leaving Page with one thought. *Dean's death wasn't from natural causes.*

CHAPTER 6

"Aren't we having the best time?" Betsy pulled a tissue from her pocket and dabbed her eyes. "All because you wanted to check out Steve's tail. You and these blasted inklings. I'm doomed to get sucked into another murder mystery solving."

Page's laugh was stuck inside. "It's telltales and not Steve's tail. I'm sorry, Bets. Really, I am. You've understood how my gift worked since we were teenagers. It's what I'm tasked to do." Page put her arm around Betsy's shoulders. "Listen, maybe Dean died from a heart attack."

Betsy sniffed. "Right. A heart attack caused by a bullet fired into his chest. You got the inkling and probably one of those strong nudges to walk over to the marina. I know you did. We're in the soup, kiddo. My gut says with some dastardly types."

"You're correct, Betsy. On this, we agree." Page craned her neck and saw Steve's black SUV pull into the parking lot. She expected Detective Koch and the forensic team would be along soon.

"You know what I'm hating the most besides the fact that the poor schmuck on the bench is dead? Want a tissue? It's my last." Betsy blew her nose.

Page shook her head. "Tell me what you hate the most."

The ad said something about a cipher. That means

math. I hate math, and it hates me right back. I see my future, and I'm not a fan. You're going to force me into poxy number hell with this case." Betsy tossed the tissue in the bin. "Here's Detective Dreamboat coming up the jetty. More fun."

"Well, snoops, what have you managed to get yourselves entangled in here? I left you tucked safely at Hibiscus Cottage after an enjoyable evening. And yet I stand ten feet away from what I assume is a dead body since you didn't ask for an ambulance." Steve's tone dripped out as 'exasperated detective.'

"All we did was take a perfectly innocent bike ride, and this is what we get—. Give me your handkerchief, Detective Tanner." Betsy gave a huff.

Steve pulled it from his back pocket. "Here ya go. I came prepared from experience." Steve looked toward the body. "Excuse me for a moment while I introduce myself to this unlucky fellow. Don't leave. You know the drill."

"Yeah, we know the drill." Page motioned to Betsy. "Let's park ourselves on the bench by the wash sink."

Within minutes, Detective Koch appeared with the team. He walked straight past Page and Betsy, offering a curt nod. The cousins watched the detectives evaluate the scene. Yellow tape was being strung to protect any evidence left behind.

"I'm not a bit happy right now." Betsy folded her handkerchief and laid it on her knee. "And we're about to get a grilling. If Koch behaves like the other times when we happened on a body, it won't be pleasant. In my current mood, he'd better not call me the Shell Isle Snoop. I swear I'll wallop Koch across his big—"

"Across my big what, Ms. Ross?" Koch stood behind Betsy, wearing a solemn expression. "That sounded like threatening an officer of the law."

Steve stood next to the other detective. His hand covered the grin, threatening to escape.

Betsy caved. "No threatening here. I'm a law-abiding citizen. I was just saying I'd appreciate it if you would use my given name."

"I think I just did. May I proceed with my questions?" Koch opened his tablet.

Page elbowed Betsy to answer.

"Sure. Fire away," Betsy replied and got another jab from Page. "Sorry, wrong word choice. Ask your questions, but I don't know much. I'm not the one who gets the inklings and nudges and lands us in these messes. I'm the poor soul who's always at the wrong place at the wrong time with said cousin."

Page let out a groan.

Betsy delivered an elbow back to Page's ribs.

Koch waved his arm in the air. "Enough from you, Ms. Ross."

"Great. Does that mean I can get my bike and ride home?" Betsy shifted on the bench like she was going to stand.

Koch turned to Steve. "This snoop has stepped on my last nerve. They're all yours to handle. I'll oversee the body removal and cleanup. That's the easy job next to their questioning."

"Sure, I've got it. We'll meet up later for the briefing."

Steve waited until Koch left before turning his eyes to Betsy. "Let's get after this. You won't wear me down like you did Koch."

Betsy hung her head in mock shame. "I'll behave."

"That'll never happen." Steve activated his phone's recorder. "Ms. Ross, do you agree to have this conversation recorded on September 22, at approximately eleven forty-five p.m.?"

"Yes." Betsy passed Steve his handkerchief and sat up straight.

"Please tell me what you know about the victim and any details regarding tonight."

"The only interaction I've had with Mr. No Personality — sorry, Dean — is when he visited Honey Bees to get a dozen popovers for the math department. There wasn't any chit-chat. He just placed his order, paid, and left. Thus, the name Mr. No Personality. This morning, Page had to go and get all snoopy, I mean interested in Dean's doings at The Perk. Better to ask her for details. I've got second-hand information. As for tonight, it was Page's blasted nudge that landed us here to discover Dead Dean. That's all from me. Well, except I know he was shot in the chest."

"Yes, I suspect the heart. And keep that fact to yourself." Steve turned his attention to Page. "You're up, Sherlocka. Don't start in the middle as you usually do. Take me back to your first sighting."

Page watched as they wheeled Dean past. She swallowed and turned to Steve. "This morning at The Perk, I saw him seated at a table alone. His face was familiar, but I couldn't place him until Betsy said he is…was a customer."

"Okay, then why don't you start with what you observed at The Perk and end with where we are right now?" Steve squatted down in front of Page.

For the next few minutes, Page laid out the events that led her to discover Dean on the bench. "So, you've got everything but my assessment. Interested, Detective Tanner?"

Betsy released a loud sigh, which was ignored.

Steve's eyes glinted. "You know I'm a believer in your inklings and keen mystery-solving abilities. Assess me, Sherlocka."

"I don't know what the cipher is all about. Clearly, the classified ads were essential to his movements."

Betsy chirped up. "You might want to note Knuckles is Page's name for the creep at The Perk. We don't know his real name. Just saying."

"Duly noted. Thank you, Betsy." Steve motioned for the women to scoot down on the bench. "My surfing knee is talking. Let me sit next to you. Page, please continue."

"As I said, I think Knuckles was after Dean for other reasons. I'm baffled by the exchange of laptops at The Perk. All I know for sure is that I got tapped into this case. Betsy and I will help in any way we can. Won't we, Bets?" Page squeezed her cousin's hand.

Betsy puffed up. "We will not. We've got Honey Bees to run. It's the harvest season, and I want to devote my energy to pumpkin—"

"Ignore her and the pumpkin chatter. She'll come around." Page folded her arms.

Steve nodded. "This is the place where I remind you two that murder is a dangerous business. You're to avoid any and all snooping that puts you in danger. Any kind of danger. Share your inklings, but don't act on them. Am I making myself heard?"

"Yep, loud and clear. The plan works for me. No snooping. Inklings go right to you. Avoid danger. Focus on Honey Bees instead." Betsy stood. "Can we please and thank you go home now?"

"Hang on. Page, I'd like your answer." Steve waited.

"I heard every word you said." Page rose. "How about you give us a ride home? Our bikes can go on your surfboard rack."

"Good idea. I fear I've lost the pedal in me," replied Betsy.

"Page?" Steve's voice sounded impatient.

"Oh, all right. We'll avoid danger, and I'll tell you when an inkling comes. In turn, you will consider allowing us to attend the interrogations of these motley suspects. Deal?" Page put out her hand.

Steve hugged her to him. "Deal, Sherlocka. What can I say? I'm putty. Let's get you two snoops—sleuths—home."

Page glanced back at the now-empty boat slip. She'd held that bit of information from Steve. It would serve a purpose later. For now, she had two suspects placed at the scene that she couldn't risk bolting. She'd ignore the guilt of omission and honor her proven methods to identify the murderer. More inklings would soon guide her next steps.

CHAPTER 7

Page stared out her bedroom window, taking in a perfect beach day. The sun's rays made the ocean sparkle like a fairy had dusted it with sparkles. She watched the lifeguard drag his chair closer to the water's edge. The number of early swimmers proved that the ocean was still inviting. Page studied the fluffy white clouds lacking any hint of gray. "That's what I like to see on my day off." She slipped on her lemon-yellow one-piece bathing suit and matching coverup. Time to face Betsy's breakfast. A concerning aroma had wafted into her bedroom.

Betsy sat at the island, thumbing through the newspaper.

"Morning. Where did you get the paper?" asked Page.

"Oh, Barnacle brought it along with his breakfast appetite. He's on the porch waiting for us to get something whipped up." Betsy's head motioned in the dog's direction.

"Uh oh. Steve's going to get chapped once he discovers Barnacle has escaped again. Still, having his paper to peruse is nice." Page laughed, seeing the dog leaving fur in Betsy's hammock.

"Start your day off with a cup of my latest coffee blend." Betsy pointed to the waiting empty mug.

"What's in this blend?" Page frowned, poured half a

cup, and sniffed before taking a tiny sip.

Betsy glanced up from the paper. "Let's see. I started with a lovely French dark roast, which I purchased from The Perk. I added a dash of cloves, a splash of guava syrup, and hazelnut coconut creamer. I think this is my new favorite Betsy Blend. Don't you agree the cloves set the fall mood? What does your taster say?"

Page took another sip, trying to get past the cloves dominating her java. "I say no one creates a morning coffee like you, Betsy Ross. Would you like for me to make breakfast? Since Ina and Daisy are running Honey Bees on slow Tuesdays, we can have a leisurely breakfast."

"No need. I've got a breakfast casserole in the oven. The timer will go off pretty soon. Take a seat." Betsy scooted the empty stool away from the island.

Page sighed and perched on the stool. The aroma confirmed her fear. The antacids would soon chase Betsy's breakfast casserole. "Did the murder make the front page?"

"How about if it didn't make any page?" Betsy rolled the paper back into its deliverable shape. "Barnacle, you owe me for getting your slobber dried off and making Steve's paper look presentable."

"Whoof."

"You're welcome." Betsy laughed.

Page touched her forehead, pondering. "Why wouldn't Dean's death make the paper? Maybe Koch and Steve are keeping this under wraps for a few hours. I guarantee you those two are plotting something, and we need to find out what."

"No, we don't. We've been told to lay low. And I'm going to do just that in about an hour. Yep, ole Betsy is going to lay herself low on the beach lounger close to that cute lifeguard. Hot flash coming. Gotta get my fan." Betsy scurried down the hall.

"Serves you right for choosing the lifeguard over helping me." Page doubted her cousin heard. The casserole's aroma sent Page to the porch in time to see Steve heading their way. "Prepare for battle stations, Barnacle."

"Barn, I figured I'd find you here mooching. Sorry about this uninvited visitor." Steve closed the screen door and pulled the dog off the hammock.

"You know Barnacle is always welcome at Hibiscus." Page took in her neighbor's muscular legs exposed by the black swim trunks. The white t-shirt emblazoned with the words 'Surf the Big Ones' testified to his sport of choice. A token ball cap tilted back gave him a rakish kind of charm. Steve Tanner might be in his early fifties, but he looked ageless.

"Did I pass inspection?" The sideways grin complemented the rake.

"Very funny. I was simply wondering how many surfing shirts you owned. I don't think I've ever seen the same one twice. Page ignored the flush creeping toward her face.

Betsy reappeared, interrupting the banter. "Hey, Steve. Join us for breakfast. I'll set an additional place at the table.

Steve looked confused at the three placemats. "I see — "

"We need a fourth. You forget Barnacle arrived before you." Betsy laughed. "Excuse me while I pull the casserole from the oven. Everyone, take a seat."

Steve whispered to Page, "What's in the casserole?"

"Search me. That's why I'm getting us extra napkins and why Barnacle is always welcome. He's great at scoffing under the table."

"My poor sucker of a dog." Steve pulled out Page's chair.

Barnacle hopped into the seat. His paper plate waited on the placemat.

"I don't believe this. He's got an assigned chair?" Steve shook his head.

Betsy returned with the dish and a large spoon. "Yep, because he kept leaving hair on my cushion. We've remedied that problem. Haven't we, Barnacle?"

"Woof." The dog licked his mouth, watching Betsy spoon a serving of casserole on Steve's plate. She deposited a few strips of crumbled bacon on the dog's plate.

"So, what have we here?" Steve suspended his fork in the air, waiting for Betsy to finish serving everyone.

Page kicked him. He nodded and reached under the table for the extra napkins she passed.

"Tuck in, you two. This dish is meant to be hearty. Sadly, the original recipe lacked punch. I took care of that easily enough," said Betsy.

"Yes, you excel at punching those recipes. What's in today's casserole?" Page peered closely at her plate. Her fork touched the too-generous serving with an extra helping of concern.

"I call it Breakfast Pep in Your Step. The main ingredients are purple potatoes, Vidalia onions, blue cheese, bacon, capers, jalapeños, of course, and my secret herbs." Betsy took a bite and looked heavenward. "So glad I added the capers and peppers to pep it up."

Page nodded and put her napkins to quick use, wishing she could swap plates with Barnacle.

"Yep, plenty of pep here." Steve's napkin followed Page's lead. "Since I'm here, guess I should earn this…hearty breakfast. This is where you two usually pepper — sorry, Page — me with questions. But I also expect some quid pro quo." Steve's hand motioned for the sleuths to engage.

"I don't have any quid for you, but Page might have some pro to quo about." Betsy laughed loudly at her word play and got rewarded by a hot flash. "Just great. Now a belly laugh ignites flashes."

"Bets, I don't think it's the laugh, but maybe what you're eating." Page pointed to the jalapeños on the plate.

"Ya think?" Betsy looked at the three stems. "Maybe I did tuck them in a little too briskly." A loud burp escaped. "Oh, dear. Excuse me for a moment."

"Quick, Steve, leave a little left on your plate and dump the rest in the napkins," instructed Page, as she set to work doing the same.

"I like the way you think. Here's mine. What are you going to do with this mess?" Steve watched Page run to the kitchen trash can and close the lid.

"Deed done. Now, when she comes back, pretend to be chewing your last bite and then compliment her. Make sure you don't overdo the bragging, or she'll make this godawful concoction again. Got it?"

"Got it. You've got this drill down pat." Steve chuckled and pushed back from the table.

"It's called survival of the mentally fittest. Shh, she's coming. Chew."

Betsy reclaimed her seat but not her plate. "I fear I may have overdone it a smidge. You were about to tell us some quo, Detective Dre...Tanner."

Steve's eyebrow raised. "I'll let pass whatever name was about to slide. Yes, I figured you'd like to know the man's identity, according to his wallet cards, is one Dean Harold Westin from Chapel, New Jersey."

"He needs Chapel now. Doesn't he?" Betsy quipped. "Sorry, those peppers and herbs awakened some stray neurons. I'm quite the wit this morning."

Page crossed her eyes at Betsy. "Moving along. What else can you share, Steve?"

"I've got an appointment at the high school with the principal and the math department head. Dean's residence is a rented beach condo. We're looking at its contents and hoping we turn up the laptop and cell phone. The medical examiner's report won't be complete for a few days, and toxicology will take a couple of weeks."

"Sounds to me like you don't have any leads." Betsy reached for her fan and lifted the hair off her neck.

"No real leads...yet. They'll come as always." Steve watched Barnacle head to the hammock. "Tell me, Sherlocka. Have you any additional insights?"

Page stood. "I think we need to scour the classifieds for the next few days for clues about the next meeting. That's our best hope to—"

Steve turned toward Page. "Hope to what?" He followed her to the foyer table.

"Hope to discover some solid leads. Here's your paper. Let's see if the morning edition has anything for us." Page searched for the classified section.

Betsy joined them. "If I was interested in this case—which I'm not—you're forgetting a piece of info that's important."

"And that is?" Page paused.

"Why isn't Dean's death reported in the paper?" Betsy retied the belt on her printed sunflower crop pants.

"Yeah, good question, Bets." Page looked at Steve expectantly.

"Oh, that. Yes, we've got our flush plan activated." Steve took the paper from Page and glanced at the name on the label. "Hang on. This is my newspaper. Why do you have my morning paper?"

Page grinned and pointed to the tooth marks and smeared ink on the front page. "Detect it for yourself."

"Barnacle! Get in here. We're going home for another disciplinary talk."

Betsy tapped Steve's forearm. "What in the world is a 'flush plan?'"

The detective's cell phone chimed. "Catch you up later, ladies," Steve answered his call and opened the door. Barnacle ran out ahead, tail dragging.

"Guess I'm going to have to wait to learn about flush plans. Ready for your beach chair? I'll load the cooler with some drinks," offered Betsy.

"What about your bathing suit?" Page followed her cousin to the kitchen.

"It's under my crops and top. I can shimmy out in a second. Hurry up. The day's wasting." Betsy pulled out the ice bin and opened the cooler.

"Okay, but can you please pack me boring snacks and drinks? You know, chips and cola," begged Page.

"Where's the fun in cola and chips? It's time you stretched your tastebuds." Betsy went to the refrigerator, humming.

Page watched a jug of neon green juice appear from the fridge and panicked. She grabbed two cans of ginger ale. "Here. Throw these in. I almost forgot to walk this envelope out to the mailbox."

"You've got two minutes. Aunt Tilly's hateful cuckoo clock says nine on the dot. We pull out at—"

"Yeah, yeah. I can make it." Page closed the front door and took a deep inhale of the salt air. She and Betsy had loved Shell Isle since they were little girls. Their mothers, being twins, managed to carve out six weeks each summer for an overseas trip and leave their girls with Aunt Tilly for the summer. They called it "Twinning Time."

Page and Betsy loved staying at Hibiscus. Shell Beach had watched them grow up and even get their first kiss under the pier. The memories were sweet and savored.

Strolling to the mailbox, Page saw a dark vehicle with tinted glass pull up. The same two faces she'd seen at the marina slipping away stared out the open window.

CHAPTER 8

"Page Wright, step closer, or if you prefer, join us inside the vehicle?" The tone of the woman's voice was colder than a polar icecap.

A shiver traveled up Page's spine. "Excuse me, but I'm late and can't imagine why you want to talk to me." Page turned toward the cottage.

The door opened. In a flash, she felt a strong hand stop her movement. "You're acting unwise," said the gruff male voice. "Now turn around and listen to what the woman has to say, and we'll be on our way."

"Okay." Page did as he requested, and the hand released her. She watched him climb into the driver's side.

The woman kept her sunglasses on, but raised her voice an octave to be heard. "Ms. Wright, it's in your best interest to forget anything or anyone you think you saw last evening at the marina. Are we clear?"

Page swallowed. "We're clear."

"Will you please hurry, Page? Your two minutes are up!" hollered Betsy from the front porch.

Relief washed over Page as the vehicle pulled away. She walked toward a waiting Betsy.

"Who was that?" Betsy's eyes followed the black SUV, quickly turning the corner.

"Just Dean's possible murderers. I'm ready to hit the beach." Page walked past a slack-jawed Betsy. "Shut your yap before a bee flies in and dies a painful death from your jalapeño breath."

Betsy closed and locked the cottage's door. "I don't know whether to feel more offended or afraid right this minute." She peered out the kitchen window. "I guess they're gone. Sheez, Page, treat yourself to a few deep breaths while I ring Steve. You've got some fast explaining to do."

"Don't you dare call him. I need time to think." Page disappeared.

Betsy went to the porch. Craning her neck to look next door, she caught sight of Steve carrying his surfboard toward the beach. "Hey, Page! Dreamboat's going surfing. From past experience, I know how this story ends. Get a move on."

"Let's go. Cut the wisecracks. What snacks did you put in that tote?" Page tried and failed to sneak a peek.

"Only good snacks. Grab your beach chair and take the cooler. We're parking next to the lifeguard. I love listening to his Ukrainian accent, and I expect to hear what just happened outside."

"You lucked out. Since I'm distracted, you won't have to explain how you're up on the lifeguard's heritage."

~*~

They set up the red-striped umbrella and matching chairs. Betsy said hello to the lifeguard and parked herself within five feet of his stand. Settled on her lounger, she turned to Page. "I'm not waiting another second. What's with the vehicle showing up? I knew you left something out last night, but I was too tired to push. Spill it, sista."

"I was waiting for the right time to tell you." Page unfolded her towel.

"Now's good. I'm going to assume you didn't enlighten Dreamboat either." Betsy popped the lid on a bottle of green tea.

"You're all about green drinks today." Page grinned, looking at the bottle of neon liquid in the cooler.

"Stop waltzing me. I don't like to dance now that I'm no longer a svelte gazelle."

"I saw the same two people last night at the marina. Unfortunately, now I know they saw me. I don't know how they found out who I was so fast. That has awakened the must-act observant radar."

"Ya think? So, do you know them? If you say yes, I'm going back to the cottage and getting my stress reduction herbal tablets. And, to think I only put them safely back in the cabinet last week. I thought we were going to have a quiet fall getting to bake pumpkin goodies."

"I know, Betsy, and I'm really sorry we've got a new case. Take heart. Maybe we can wrap it quickly." Page reached over and squeezed her cousin's hand.

"Let me hear the bad news so I can mentally escape with the dowager. I want to hide in the pretend world of the seventeen hundreds and forget about Dead Dean." Betsy pulled her book out.

Page devoted the next fifteen minutes to explaining the details of the prior evening's sightings. She watched Betsy gulp air, unable to talk. The flash fan worked overtime. "So, now you know everything I do."

Betsy found her voice. "I don't like any of it either. All four of these reprobates seem capable of killing. I can't think about any of this right now." Betsy rolled out of her lounger.

"Where you going?" asked Page

"To down my bottle of stress reducers. Then, I'm coming back to read my book and ignore you. Don't you dare try to change my mind." Betsy marched toward the cottage.

"Nope. It's a good plan," Page muttered and felt a little less frazzled. Betsy was her comic relief.

She let her mind enjoy the distraction of watching Steve surf. Page marveled at how he could own each wave. The swells were building from the sandbar, forming an impressive height and break line. Steve managed to stay ahead of the curve on his current ride. "You scored a ten on that wave," said Page to no one.

"I'm back. What did you just say?" asked Betsy, arranging herself in the chair.

"Nothing, I was talking to myself. Get with the dowager like you planned. By the way, how does she like her summer on the Cornish coast? A bit rocky, I hear." Page grabbed the sunscreen and applied more to her face.

"She's having issues with the kitchen staff and the menu for next week's gala. I can barely abide reading what she'd chosen to serve. So blah."

"You should reach out to the author and offer her culinary counseling," teased Page.

"Why, yes, that's a wonderful idea. I'll do that tonight because we'll be home. And that means you will not get any inklings. What does Steve want? He's waving to us."

Page glanced in his direction and waved. He was sitting on the board, motioning and smiling.

"Oh, silly me. I know that come hither look he's sending your way, and that's how the story ends. Poor ole Betsy sitting alone while her cousin swims out to her Adonis."

Page laughed and stood up. "Well, poor ole Betsy, didn't you want me to tell Steve about my visitors? When he's on the water, he's all chill, and right now, I need him to chill. Back in a few minutes."

The water felt bracing on Page's skin. Fall had decided to drop the day's air and water temperature. Page dove into the ocean. Her arms made long strokes toward the bobbing yellow surfboard. She came alongside the board, "You rang?"

Steve offered his hand and hoisted Page next to him. His face wore a 'don't mess with me' expression. "You bet I rang, Sherlocka. Want to tell me about your visitors this morning?"

"I figured your nosy self didn't miss the exchange. I was waiting for the right time to tell you." Page repositioned herself on the surfboard. "Big mother wave coming. Don't you dare let me get swallowed like the other day. My throat still burns from the gallons of water I drank."

Steve's grin appeared. "Your throat burns because of what Betsy feeds you. Lay down. I'm going to paddle out further."

Page put a death grip on the side of the board as the mother wave lifted them toward the heavens. "Paddle faster. I don't want an encore of that ride. The waves are getting larger, and the wind has picked up. Maybe I'd rather have this conversation on land."

"Relax. We're good out here. The faster you talk, the sooner I'll take you to shore." Steve wiped the water droplets from Page's cheek.

The intimate gesture took her breath away. It felt more like a caress. She refused to look at his sapphire eyes. "Okay, but promise you won't lecture me?"

"No can do. What facts have you held back, and who were those people in the vehicle? Answer those two questions, and you'll be in your lounger feeding Betsy's lunch to the seagulls in minutes. Or we do this officially, like at the station. You choose, Page."

"Sounds good. So, I happened to catch a glimpse of two people at the marina last night. They came out of the shadows and left on a boat. We'd just discovered Dead Dean, as Betsy calls him." Page paused to consider her next words.

"Okay, but that doesn't mean these two people had anything to do with the murder." Steve adjusted the surfboard's position as the next set of waves approached. He studied Page. "What's their connection?"

"They were the same pair who paid me a visit earlier, bringing a message."

"And that message would be? I swear I should have been a dentist?" Steve's exasperation was evident.

"A dentist? I don't understand—"

"Getting information from you is like pulling teeth."

"Ha. Aren't you funny? As I was getting to, they warned me to forget anything or anyone I might have seen.

Betsy came outside, and they took off." Page wished she'd told the story in a different order.

"You caught sight of a couple at the scene who tracked you down and delivered a threat? I'll need any descriptions you can give for the two. Before I replay my lecture about holding things back, is there more?" Steve waited.

"Don't get worked up, but I kind of saw them when we were at Movie on the Green."

"You saw these people and didn't see fit—"

"I see fit now to tell you. I didn't want to risk you and Koch scaring them off before we could figure out their racket. This idea seemed perfectly logical to me last night. Maybe not so much at this moment." Page dropped her head, signaling remorse.

"If there's one thing I've learned after working two murder cases with you, it's that every decision, every move is calculated. You delight in feeding me a few morsels and use the rest as bargaining chips. And, if that's mixing metaphors, I don't care. Start with your first encounter and bring me to where we're now sitting on my surfboard."

"I knew you'd react this way...all FBI pushy and condescending. That's why I like to work alone with Betsy." Page noticed Steve's clenched jaw. "Fine. I got an inkling last night and did the popsicle run to act on it. I walked toward the pavilion, and Dean was having a rough go with three people."

"Describe them." Steve paused. "Please."

"The leader they called Jewel was probably in her fifties with dark hair. What a jewel this woman seemed, only a rough cut. No polish. Cold as ice. The guy they called Lucky acted as her do-boy. I'd describe him as a ginger, stocky, and a hitman type. He comes off as intimidating. How am I doing?"

"You'll get your grade after we're done. Keep going." Steve waved to an approaching surfer. "Paddle with me. I don't want interruptions."

"Paddle? We're not going to ride a wave in? That didn't go well for me last time. I fell off as the wave broke. Skinned my knees on the sandy bottom." Page watched as Steve gauged the next set of waves.

"On your belly. We're going. Enjoy the ride." Steve paddled faster and stood, maneuvering around a stretched-out Page.

The curl's spray teased her body as she watched in awe as Steve teased it back. "Can I try standing?"

"Sure, but hurry, or you'll miss the ride." Steve's hand steadied Page until she'd gained balance. "Bend your knees. That's right."

"Oh my gosh, I'm in love." They entered the shallow water and jumped off the surfboard.

He wiped the water from his eyes. "Wow, I didn't expect to hear this so early in our relationship."

"Cut it out. You know what I mean. I want to learn to surf. Am I too old? Wait, I'm younger than you." Page glanced at her body. "Still, I'm hardly firm. I'm rethinking my declaration."

"We can revisit your declaration another time. Stand here with me and finish your confession." Steve's hand kept the board close.

"Okay. Stella acted like Dean's girlfriend. She took up for him when the others threatened his ability to walk the earth. Stella had long, blond, wavy hair and clanky jewelry."

"What the heck is clanky jewelry?" A smile tugged at Steve's lips.

"You know. Bangle bracelets that make noise. Forget that part. Listen, Stella had an accent I couldn't place. Come to think of it, Jewel had a slight accent, too."

"Nice observation. Could you ascertain what Dean had done to warrant Jewel and Lucky's wrath?"

"Yep. He wanted out of whatever they were involved in doing. Dean backed down fast once he realized his mistake. Stella talked Jewel into giving Dean a chance to prove loyal by letting him handle last night's exchange. That pretty much sums up what I witnessed."

Steve lifted his sunglasses and gazed into Page's aqua eyes. "Which brings us to the big reveal, pretty lady. Who did you see at the marina? Who visited you?"

"Lucky and Stella."

"Hmm, not Jewel?" Steve stared out at the line of surfers.

"Nope. Call it an unexpected fact that's been chasing my logical mind. Stella is or was Dean's squeeze. Yet, she's cavorting around with Lucky. It doesn't add up, but this murder is all about numbers and ciphers, which don't add up either." Page hopped when she felt something under water brush her leg.

"Where are you going? We're not done." Steve reached for Page's hand.

"I'm going to the shallows. Someone tried to make friends." Page pointed into the water.

Steve chuckled and followed. "You do realize that it's imperative for you and Betsy not to meddle in this case? We don't have the identities or location of this group, so surveillance on them is nil for now. I'm going to assign a plain clothes officer to you. At least I'll relax knowing—"

"I don't want some guy on my tail day in and day out. That'll make more trouble if those people see the police guarding me. Don't you see? I need to play this down. Like I'm busy living my life and moving on. Right?" Page's voice sounded pleading to her ears. "I'm seasoned as a sleuth, Steve. Trust me and my instincts."

"If something happened to you, I'd—"

Page grabbed his hand. "Trust my intuition. Trust my process. It keeps me safe. Okay?"

"Okay, I'll take it under advisement." Steve hugged her to him.

Page caught sight of Betsy moving their way. "She's on the move."

"Yep, and so am I. Surfs up." Steve grabbed his board.

"Just swell. She's waving the lunch sack. I'm doomed."

Grinning, Steve tapped Page's shoulder. "Hang on. How about a sail around six tonight? You'll get out of dinner with Betsy, and I'll have you under my watch."

"I'm your first mate. See ya later, assuming I survive lunch."

CHAPTER 9

Betsy exited her bedroom wearing a bright turquoise Mermaids Bowling Team shirt and jeans. Her auburn hair was secured by a tortoise shell clip, but the red tomato shade of lipstick stole the show. "Guess I'm ready to knock some pins down. Eh, cousin?"

"Yep, you're a real knock-out tonight," Page said with a little twist to her lips.

"Why do I think those words have a double meaning?" Betsy glanced in the hall mirror at her countenance and puckered her lips. "Betsy Ross, you're one ravishing broad. Tonight, you shall attract male attention. Your purgatory on avoiding all men has ended."

"So it has, hot lips," said Page. "I put your bowling bag by the door."

"Thanks. You know I wouldn't go bowling with Ina and the gals if you didn't have plans with Dreamboat. After your little tête-à-tête this morning, we need to be extra careful out and about. I'm jittery about this case."

"Don't worry about me. Steve's the best protector I could ask for. You'll be with a group, which is a good thing. Fortunately, you're not the one they've taken a shine to." Page tied the aqua cotton tee's matching scarf into a nautical knot.

"I'm holding onto those words," said Betsy.

"With any luck, the trio has moseyed to another town. That's Ina honking. Go crush those pins, Mermaid Betsy." Opening the door, Page waved to Ina and saw Steve heading her way.

Barnacle reached her first and dropped his wet chew stick on her sneakers.

"You're too generous, Barn. You keep it." Page kicked the stick back his way.

"Having your appetizer early? Barnacle, get the bone off the porch and go home." Steve accepted the beach bag from Page. "You look nice tonight. The color blue makes your eyes come alive, or maybe it's the company you keep?" Steve's lips brushed her cheek.

"Could be the company, but it's probably the shirt," Page teased back. The kiss woke up her flutters. "Hang on while I grab the brownies I baked for us. I hid them to ensure their survival from a certain someone's sweet tooth."

"Nuts?" asked Steve.

"Nuts? I wouldn't go so far as to say Bets is nuts because she —" Steve popped the SUV's hatch.

"Are there nuts in the brownies?"

Page entered the passenger side, laughing. "Pecans. Lots of them, and dark chocolate morsels."

Steve's eyes swept up and down Page's body. "I vote brownies for our first course, and after that...we'll see."

~*~

As Page and Steve walked toward Carpe Diem, she noticed the evening air possessed a kind of gloominess. It was as if the breeze carried the memory of Dean's life-ending a hundred yards away. She glanced around the floating dock, taking in the scene.

A group of men hoisted ice chests onto a fishing boat, placing bets on who'd catch the biggest snapper. *Nothing concerning there,* Page thought. She observed a couple with two young children enjoying a picnic on their small cutter. Her eyes scanned the next row of power boats. Silence surrounded them. Everything appeared normal, but it was illusory. A murderer moved about Shell Isle. She sensed a presence. Were they being watched? Steve's voice called her back.

"Ahoy, first mate." Steve unclipped the line blocking the entrance. "Step aboard."

"I'm stepping," Page answered.

"Let's stow our dinner and things below. The wind's shifting to the south, which is a good omen for our night sailing."

"Aye, aye, I know the drill, Captain Steve." The corners of Page's mouth turned up.

Steve pulled her close. "I don't know whether to kiss you or—"

"Definitely, the kiss." Page stood on tiptoes, pressed her lips against his, and disappeared below.

"Good choice," Steve hollered down.

Page returned to the deck, untied the lines, and signaled Steve to cast off. Once the sailboat's auxiliary engine came to life, she claimed the bow seat. Steve wouldn't need help until they got into open water. Page enjoyed the sea's chatter against Carpe's hull for the next few minutes. The sound was almost musical with a beat of its own. Once Page saw they'd cleared the marina, she approached the mainsail's boom and began releasing ties.

"Here, let me get these." Steve's forearm muscles flexed as he worked.

Page sucked in a breath, telling her mind to focus on her first mate duties. "I'll stand by to unfurl the jib." She readied the small sail and watched Steve return to the helm.

He positioned Carpe Diem to eat the wind, killed the engine, and let the mainsail loose. The sail billowed for a few seconds before catching the breeze. Steve signaled Page to unfurl the smaller sail at the front of the boat.

Within seconds, the wind filled both sails, and Page joined Steve at the wheel. "I think we're about to have a fantastic—"

"Steady there, best mate." Steve grabbed Page. "Carpe loves to lean over into the water and let the wind propel her."

Page's grin widened as exhilaration claimed her. "Ya know something, Captain Steve?"

"Tell me, Calypso," Steve answered, in reference to the mythological character and the island they liked to sail to.

"Nothing feels like the thrill of heeling over when Carpe's sails fill. Boy, is she rocketing our speed tonight. What's the hurry, you two?" Page stayed on the windward side and grabbed hold of the railing.

"For me, it's hunger!" Steve hollered over the wind. "I can't speak for Carpe Diem."

"Nor should you ever speak for a woman."

"Listen, there's a small island I want to show you. I

thought we might drop anchor and dine on the beach. Sound okay by you?"

"Sounds perfect." Page saw his maneuver and shifted position.

"Duck. We're coming about. Island is on your left."

The sun put on a final color show to close its shift for the day. Shades of orange and indigo washed the sky as the sailboat entered a private lagoon. Two boats were anchored nearby, ready to receive the scuba divers. Cameras dangled from their arms as they climbed aboard their boats.

"There's a reef a few hundred yards away. It's been getting attention lately from this diving group. They're freelance photographers for international magazines. "I hope you have a bathing suit hiding somewhere. Time to wade to shore." Steve held up their dinner tote and a blanket.

Page peeled off her jeans and top, revealing a melon-colored bathing suit. "Let's do this. After Betsy's disastrous lunch of mock curry chicken salad, I'm hungry enough to eat seaweed. Plus, I'm hoping you'll update me on the case."

~*~

Stretched out on the blanket, Page watched Steve put away their empty sushi boxes. She'd come to savor their outings and time together. No ties to bind were how she viewed things. The ideal romance at this point in their lives.

Steve joined her but said nothing.

Page looked his way. His eyes were fixed on the heavens. "So, are you pondering the cosmos or escaping there with your thoughts?" She sat up and touched his arm.

"Are you making a move on me?" Steve reached for

her hand and bestowed a kiss.

She grinned at the gallant gesture. "Perhaps. Perhaps not the move you'd like. Answer my question without teasing and flirting, Captain."

Steve turned on his side, propping his head on his hand. "I don't flirt. I act."

Page tossed her head back. "Oh, I think you do both and very well. Answer, please."

"Okay, I was thinking how since you opened Honey Bees, I see so little of you. Combined with the fact that Betsy is still ensconced at Hibiscus, probably forever."

Page groaned. "I know. Things have been hectic. And Betsy—"

"Is always around us. No duenna walks the earth more diligently than Betsy Ross when it comes to chaperoning you. She's kept our hanky-panky at zero. Zip. Flatlined." Steve paused. "Now you know what's on my mind."

Page scooted closer to her detective, her captain, maybe even her guy. "I've got the hanky if you brought the panky." As she tilted her chin to receive his kiss, Steve's cell phone rang.

"Just great. I'm about to score hanky and this blasted thing—Tanner here."

Laying her head on his chest, a smile spread across her face. Her nose caught a whiff of his masculine scent. Sea air mixed with some citrus aftershave was intoxicating. Judging by his words, their timing was off. She needed distance, but his arm wrapped around her as she tried to sit upright.

"What time are you releasing? I'll be there. Anything

preliminary from the ME? Thanks, Koch." Steve tossed the cell phone on the blanket and wrapped his other arm around Page. "Come here, you."

"I assume we have to pull up anchor, Captain?" Page rested her chin on his shoulder.

"Yeah, we do. I can't blame this one on your cousin." Steve drew his hands down her silky hair. "We're activating our plan to flush out the murderer. Before we shove off, I have a more imperative mission." Steve's lips found Page's. For the next few minutes, hanky met panky.

CHAPTER 10

Steve and Page sailed with their disappointment back to the marina. The evening had been cut short for a reason, she applauded. They hurried to secure Carpe Diem so Steve could play his role with Koch.

Sailing home, Page learned the police hadn't garnered a single lead in locating the four suspects, which meant time was working against them. She promised again to share any inklings or information. Like the police, nothing was coming to her.

Pulling into Hibiscus driveway thirty minutes later, Steve walked Page to the door. "Assuming our flush-out plan succeeds, can I get a do-over this weekend?" His sapphire eyes settled directly on hers.

Page managed a nod.

Twisting her hair around his fingers, he whispered in her ear, "Like spun silk. Have I told you that besides those aqua eyes, the color of your hair attracted me like a bear to honey?"

Page melted a little more and licked her lips. "I don't think so."

The front door opened. "A bear to honey?" Betsy stood in the arch, hands on hips. "Is that supposed to sound romantic? A bear?"

An embarrassed Steve and Page stepped apart.

"Duenna, your timing is consistently lousy when I'm making my moves." Steve broke into laughter and kissed the top of Page's head. "Gotta dash, snoops. Stay home and safe."

Betsy looked puzzled and turned to Page. "What does he mean by calling me a duenna? Sounds Yiddish and unflattering. I'll ask Ina." Betsy held the screen door for Page to pass.

"Bring your meddlesome self inside. I've got an update on our case. It's time we strategize." Page dropped her tote on the island barstool and poured a glass of tea.

"I'm not in the mood for an update. The Mermaids lost tonight by six pens." Betsy pouted. Her red lipstick had become a memory. She settled on the wicker sofa and hugged a floral throw pillow.

Page joined her in the living room. "I hate this swivel chair as much as you hate Aunt Tilly's cuckoo clock."

Betsy made a face at the cuckoo.

Page glanced at the clock's time. "It's ten o'clock. We both had a night of exercise, so I'll make this brief. First, I'm sorry to hear the Mermaid's winning streak got busted. You're still ranked number one, right?"

"Yeah, but we've got to play the team in second place next week. Ina's convinced we can beat them as long as Eileen gets her new glasses in time."

"See there? You were disadvantaged tonight by Eileen's faulty eyesight. The Mermaids will triumph." Page sipped her tea.

"Let's hope so. Give me the condensed update on a

case I think we should steer clear of involvement. That couple gave me the worries." Betsy propped her foot on the coffee table. "Is it hot in here? Hang on. I need my pretty fan. It's a lovely shade of lavender. I should strap the things to my arm."

Page waited for Betsy to return. "All set now? Don't you want a spicy cookie or — ?"

"Not funny. Get on with the telling. I left the dowager in her soaking tub."

"Steve explained about their flush plan being activated tonight. They've kept the murder out of the papers for a clever ploy. Tonight, the story breaks that Dean Westin suffered a non-fatal gunshot wound and is recovering at the local hospital. Koch and Steve hope that the murderer will hear this and try to finish the job."

"Wow. Sounds risky to me. Who's the poor sap that has to lie in the bed pretending to be Dean?" Betsy sauntered into the kitchen.

"It's a rookie who volunteered. He had knee surgery, so laying around for a few days helps his recovery." Page twisted to see Betsy munching a cookie. "Ah, the power of suggestion. Did you sprinkle cayenne on it?"

"No, I did not sprinkle cayenne on — get over here and look out this window." Betsy killed the kitchen light.

"Not good, Bets." Page closed the blind. "Let me think."

"Think? What's to think about?" Betsy reached for her cell phone and moved away from Page. "Thank goodness you answered. I figured if you saw my number…oh, never mind. We have unwelcome guests outside Hibiscus."

Page tried and failed to grab the phone from Betsy.

"Well, make it speedy. I'm not enamored with these… hello? Hello?" Betsy laid her cell phone on the counter.

"What's happening? So you know, I was going to call Steve." Page pulled Betsy into the living room.

"Oh, there's going to be a block party in about five minutes, but we're not invited. Too bad because I have a new Mumu perfect for the occasion. It's black and white stripes. It could pass as prison garb."

Page couldn't help laughing. "Cut the cracks. I know your MO when a case of nerves hits you. I sure hope whoever is in that vehicle hangs around long enough. Maybe I should step outside—"

"Are you loopy? Too much hanky-panky has caused your brain to go mushy. Over my dead body—no—make that under no circumstances are you getting past me." Betsy hurried and plastered her body against the cottage door.

"Okay, relax." Page peeked out another window. "Damn."

"What? You never say four-letter words. You let me have them all." Betsy came to Page's side.

"The vehicle is gone. Steve and Koch lost the chance to nab them for questioning and probably make an arrest." Page wondered why there had been no further inklings.

"Your cell phone's ringing somewhere." Betsy headed toward the sound. "I got it." She took the cell to Page.

"Sure." Page moved to unlock the door. Betsy hovered like a hungry mosquito.

Steve and Koch entered with solemn faces.

"You missed them. The block party got canceled." Betsy grabbed a breath. "Yep, I love my life at Shell Isle. So stimulating. So life-threatening." Betsy parked herself and her sarcasm on a stool.

Steve glanced around the cottage. "You two are okay, right? Page, you didn't do anything stupid like go outside—"

"Oh, she wanted to, but I stopped her," replied Betsy.

"Such a caring, blabbing duenna." Page's eyes sent daggers to her cousin.

"Again, with this duenna thing," huffed Betsy.

"Enough. May we assume you two magpies did stay inside? Other than seeing the black SUV outside, do you have anything to add?" Koch rubbed his forehead.

"Nothing." Betsy activated her fan.

"Such a missed opportunity," lamented Page.

"On that, we can all agree," Steve answered a text and clipped the phone to his belt. "After these suspects showed up here again, we need to get protection for Page—and I suppose—the chatterbox."

Koch nodded, not bothering to keep his grin inside.

"You *suppose* I need protection? *Suppose*, you big lug?" Betsy delivered a playful fist into Steve's bicep. "This duenna wants the biggest, baddest cop you've got."

"That would be me." Steve turned to Page. "I'm spending the night here."

Page opened her mouth to protest. "But—"

"No buts," said Steve.

"You won't hear a but out of me. Bring extra protection." Betsy moved toward the hall.

"What extra protection is she talking about? That sounds risqué—" offered Koch.

"I think she means the canine kind," Steve smirked. "Koch, hang around for ten minutes while I go next door and grab a few things."

"And, Barnacle!" hollered Betsy from her bedroom.

Page threw her arms in the air. "Fine. I surrender Hibiscus and my privacy to the free world. I'll get you a pillow and a blanket. You and Barnacle can sleep on Aunt Tilly's wicker sofa. It's short the extra foot you'll need to stretch out." Page disappeared.

"Seems you're not a welcome guest, Tanner." Koch opened the screen door.

"Our snoops will come around. Let's hope the others do as well. We've got to nab them at the next opportunity. At least, the net is set at the hospital." Steve jogged down the steps.

~*~

"Need anything else?" Page watched, amused, as Steve tried to position himself on the sofa. His calves and ankles hung off the end. A contented Barnacle slept on a towel next to the couch.

"I could go for a cozy tuck-me-in kiss." Steve spread his arms.

"No hot and heavy out there! I don't own enough fans. Page, go to bed!"

"Ignore her." Grinning, Steve pulled Page down next to him and delivered hot.

Page showed him her version and then jumped up

when she heard Betsy's voice again.

"I don't like what I'm not hearing. And I looked up duenna. Yours is about ready to come out there. Have a heart, you two. I live in a desert with no affection."

"Duly noted. Say goodnight, Steve." Page blew him a kiss.

"Goodnight, Steve." He rolled over and fell off the sofa, making a loud thump. Barnacle howled. "Sorry, fellow."

"What now?" hollered Betsy.

"Nothing. All is good. Barnacle and I are working out sleeping arrangements." Steve rubbed his back and crawled back on the sofa, letting his legs hang off the sofa's back. "I didn't plan on sleeping, but getting comfortable isn't too much to ask. Right, Barn?"

The dog yawned and dropped his head.

"Okay, I see how this goes, Barnacle. I'll take the first watch since I've got some research to do. Yep, there's someone else who isn't a fan of Dean Westin." Steve typed into his phone.

CHAPTER 11

Betsy padded into the kitchen and woke up the espresso machine. "Morning, detective. Give me a sec to get caffeinated and dressed for a day at Honey Bees. I'll return and whip up a delightful breakfast as a thank you for standing guard."

Bullet fast, Steve grabbed his gun and phone and made for the door. "Sorry, Betsy, duty calls. I'll take a rain check on breakfast. Tell Page to walk over in the next half hour. I've got an invite for her." He closed the screen door only to open it. "By the way, I've got a plain clothes officer sitting on the front porch glider." Steve let the door slam and jogged across the yard.

"Maybe he'd like to sample my breakfast." Betsy stepped out onto the porch. "Hey, there, handsome. Would you like to experience my famous French toast?"

The policeman, in his late fifties, approached Betsy and smiled. "I'm from Quebec, so French toast sounds great. Thank you."

"Excellent." Betsy stood like a statue and gawked at the man. "I—"

"Yes, Steve neglected to introduce us. I'm Officer Andre Lyon." He offered his hand to Betsy.

Coming back to life, Betsy accepted his shake. "Your accent is charming. Oh, I'm Betsy Ross. It's okay if you want to joke about my name."

Andre's eyes crinkled at the corners. "No, I think not. I prefer to hear about this toast you're making...though I suspect you create and don't make food. Yes?"

Betsy's head bobbed. "But how could you know this? I mean—"

"Ah, mademoiselle, you asked if I'd like to experience your toast. I would like this very much." Andre bowed.

"Oh my." Betsy's hand fluffed her hair. "Shall I bring your plate here, or would you like to join my cousin and me inside for the repast?"

"Alas, my orders are to remain here until my shift ends in four hours. It's probably better if I remain watchful outside. Another officer is to accompany you to what you call the Honey Bees?"

"Yes, Honey Bees is our specialty shop in town. We're featuring baked pumpkin items—I have a thing for pumpkin—" Betsy backed into the screen door. "Oh my. Excuse me, Officer Lyon, while I go prepare—toast—I mean French toast."

"But, of course. I shall anticipate it with great verve." Andre returned to his chair.

~*~

Page appeared in the kitchen. "I've never heard you whistle. What's that song? It sounds...French."

"I'm preparing a special French toast. I find singing enhances my creative self." Betsy reached for the hot sauce and sprinkled it liberally into the mixture. She tossed in almond slivers and cumin.

Page gulped. "Another savory French toast? It's been a while since you made—"

"Created, Page. I create." Betsy glanced toward the porch and gave a Cheshire smile.

"Sure, create. What's going on here? Where's Steve?" Page looked in the living room.

"Oh, I forgot. Dreamboat wants you to walk over. He's got an invite to bestow upon you." Betsy added goat cheese.

Seeing the latest ingredient convinced Page to make a hasty exit. "Guess I'll walk over. Maybe save me a slice of… toast." She'd figure out how to dispose of it later.

"Will do. Say hi to Andre as you leave." Betsy turned her attention to the skillet.

"Who the heck is Andre?"

Betsy pointed outside with her spatula and went back to singing.

Page gave a shrug and waltzed out the door. She stopped short and pivoted. Betsy was serious about a man being on her porch. She noted his attire of khaki pants and a navy polo shirt. "Hello. You're Andre? My cousin told me—" Page accepted his extended hand.

"Yes, I'm Andre Lyon, the officer assigned first shift to keep you safe."

Page liked his countenance, and this time recognized an accent. "It's nice to meet you, and thank you for being here. French?"

Andre nodded. "French Canadian."

Steve appeared in his front yard. "Page? Coffee's hot, and so is the news I've got waiting on you."

"Coming. See you later, Officer Lyon. Oh, a word of warning. If Betsy offers you breakfast, turn it down."

"Yes, ma'am." A frown appeared on Andre's face.

Poor man, she could tell her warning came too late. Page hurried to Steve's side.

"Morning, Sherlocka."

Page noted that the shower had just released Steve. His black hair was still damp, and he smelled like the woods. If she kept reacting like this, she'd need to invest in some of Betsy's hand fans. Page forced her mind to a safe topic. "Lead me to the coffee. I owe you big time. Betsy's making some new savory French toast recipe, and you don't want to ask what's in it. I fear that the officer's digestive system will soon succumb."

"Andre's sharp. One serving will educate him. Come inside and bring any of those tinklings."

"For pity's sake, they're inklings. Stop messing with me, or I won't agree to whatever plan you've hatched."

Steve kissed the top of her head and motioned for her to go inside the bungalow. "Have a seat. I'll pour you a cup. Want a bowl of cereal?"

"Coffee's fine for now. I'm not over the cooking aroma at my place." Page accepted the steaming espresso. "Nice brew. A hint of caramel?"

Steve nodded. "Very good. And?" He grabbed a sip before placing the mug on the end table.

"And...pecan? It's praline." Page high-fived the air. "I'm going to want a refill in a few minutes. So good, detective."

Steve did a mock bow. "Let's get to it."

Page sat up straight and let her smile fade. "Talk."

"As I told you last night, we're making little to no progress with this case. We've talked to our informants, and no one knows anyone meeting the descriptions of the four suspects. So, either they're from other places or not part of Shell Isle's dwindling low-life community."

"Sounds like a dead end."

"Yep." Steve grabbed another gulp of his espresso. "Damn, this really is good. Anyway, you know the story broke in the paper about Dean recovering in the hospital. So, that trap is set. We've tracked down where his father lives, but he's not returned our calls. It may be a stepfather because they have different last names. We ran a check on Dean's driver's license. Nothing came back suspicious there."

"Surely, his father needs to be told his son is dead."

"Surely, he does, and that's why I've called in a favor. One of my FBI buddies is going to the father's home in Chapel, New Jersey, this morning. We're hoping Mr. Mintto is there and will agree to keep quiet about his son's death for a few days."

"Maybe he was in recent communication with Dean and can tell you something of value. You'll know more soon enough. What else?" Page passed her empty cup with a grin. "More, please."

Steve returned. "Here you go. This brings us to my invitation. I've got a meeting this morning with the high school principal and head of the math department. Remember Mickey said the head wasn't a fan of Dean? I'm desperate to find anyone who didn't cotton to our victim. It's a long shot. Maybe you'd like to tag along and see if you get any hits or… inklings? Game?"

Page blew on her coffee. She had two things to discuss, but they could wait a few moments. "I'm game. Do you have any info to share about these two people we're meeting?"

"Nothing came up on the search. They're about as vanilla boring as you can get. The principal has been at the school for decades, and the department head for about four years. I doubt we'll glean much from these two. Still, it's Investigation 101 to interview the victim's employer and any peers of interest. That's all I've got for you."

Page felt Steve studying her. "What?"

"Something has put a worried frown on your face. You've got the floor. Talk to me." Steve leaned into the sofa cushions and winced. "Sorry. My accommodations last night lacked a little—"

"Watch it, buster. Aunt Tilly will come down and mess with you for disparaging her beloved wicker settee." Page laughed. "You're right. I have two things. One is a fretter, and the other a task. I'm frustrated because I can't place Jewel and Stella's accents. Knowing the answer could prove important."

"I agree. Maybe it will come to you. What else?" Steve opened the back door for Barnacle to enter.

The spaniel ran to Page and dropped his bone on her shoe again.

Steve bent down and tossed the rawhide. "Barn, the bone is your treasure. Page doesn't take to your gift."

"Hey, fellow." Page grinned and stroked the dog's

ears. "Second, I need to see the morning's classified section. I expect we'll find something there."

Steve went to the kitchen. "The paper arrived earlier. I quickly perused the story on Dean. Koch and I plan to scour the daily classifieds for clues. Here you go."

Unfolding the section, Page ran her fingers down the columns. "I do not see—wait, here's something. This could be it."

Steve sat next to her. "Read it."

"Cipher 0925-2100CS. That's all. I sense it's Dean's next assignment and tied to what I overheard at Movie on the Green."

"Problem is, Dean won't make that rendezvous, but I'm betting someone else will. Since the last meeting was likely at the marina, we can set up surveillance for this evening if the coming storm doesn't interfere."

"I suppose." Page twisted her mouth to the side, studying the ad.

"You don't seem enamored with my plan." Steve went to fill their mugs.

An inkling—though weak—came. "Forget the refills. We need to go to the high school, like now." Page rose.

"The meeting isn't for another—"

"Now, Steve."

"Now it is. Barnacle, to the backyard you go."

Page went to the front door. "I'm going to grab my handbag and let Betsy know we're leaving."

CHAPTER 12

Steve parked his SUV near the school's entrance. "We're here. What's next?"

"I'm not sure. I suppose we might see if the principal and department head are available." Page opened the passenger door, stepping out.

Steve came alongside. "Okay, Sherlocka, let's do this."

Walking a few yards, Page glimpsed a white pickup truck waiting at a stoplight on the side street a few yards away. She recognized the face and knew why she'd gotten the nudge to look. "Quick, Steve. My inkling was right. That's Knuckles in the white truck."

"What? Knuckles? Wait here." He took off running toward his SUV.

Page watched a stream of school buses entering the parking lot to drop off kids. Steve wasn't going anywhere. They'd blocked him. She watched him walk back to her, wearing a frustrated expression. She had one to match.

"Of all the damn luck. At least I called the truck in." He waved his arm in the air. "Your inkling got us here for the sighting, but fate—"

"Saw fit to let Knuckles live to cause trouble another day. Let's go see what these two academics think of Dean. Maybe we'll get something out of this morning yet." Page beamed a smile at Steve and tugged on his arm. "Come on, handsome. Dazzle me with your questioning acumen."

He tipped her chin. "Sherlocka, your wiles work on me even though I'm chapped over missing Knuckles."

Moments later, Steve had them in front of Principal Holly. Page waited for her introduction.

Steve took a chair next to Page, across from the principal's desk. "Mr. Holly, I appreciate your meeting us earlier. This is Page Wright, who consults for the police department."

Holly stacked a group of files and placed them on the corner of his desk. "How may I assist you? I regret to say I've got a busy morning."

"I'm here to ask you some questions about one of your teachers, Dean Westin."

"Ah, yes, such a tragedy he got himself injured. I read the paper. I'm going to stop by the hospital on my way home this evening." Holly leaned back in his leather chair, allowing the sun to illuminate his bald spot.

Page pinched her arm to keep from laughing.

"No visitors are allowed. I'm sure you understand. This was a gunshot wound and not self-inflicted. While Dean is unable to communicate, we have to push forward to find the person who shot him and why."

Holly gave a curt nod. "I understand. How can I help?"

"Tell me about Mr. Westin as a teacher, an employee, and what his peers think of him." Steve pulled out his phone to record the conversation. "May I?"

Page smiled at Steve's carefully chosen use of the

present tense.

"Yes, yes, of course. Mr. Westin keeps to himself, as we Brits like to say. He's what I call a ghost teacher." Holly almost smiled.

"A ghost teacher?" Steve's expression changed to confusion.

"Yes, I know he's in the building and teaching, but I never see the man moving around the halls and certainly not in the cafeteria." Holly rubbed his chin. "Fact of the matter is, I don't recall ever seeing him eat lunch. Isn't that odd?"

"Maybe he's dieting?" The words slipped out. Page mouthed, "Sorry."

Holly shook his head. "He isn't a man carrying extra weight."

"Is Mr. Westin liked by other teachers and the students?" pressed Steve.

"I'd say he isn't liked or disliked. My impression is no one really knows him to form an opinion. As for the students, I've had no complaints. A ghost teacher, like I said."

"I think I get your drift. How long has Dean been teaching? What do you know about his background? Steve checked his phone and looked at the principal.

Holly opened the file in front of him. "Let's see what I can share. I printed this a moment ago. He joined my staff over the summer, actually a few weeks before the summer session began." Holly laid his glasses to the side.

"And you needed to fill a teaching slot?" Steve leaned in.

"Why yes, I required a new math teacher, and Mr.

Westin had the credentials. I interviewed him and asked my administrator to follow the proper protocol to hire him." Holly acted pensively.

"You felt confident in your interview with him as well?" Steve pressed harder.

"Mr. Westin met the job qualifications. I see no problem here, Detective Tanner, and I'd appreciate it if you wouldn't try to create one. I'm answering your questions truthfully." Holly glanced at his wristwatch. "Now, if there isn't anything else, I have a meeting with a group of parents. They insist we add tennis to the physical education curriculum, even though the school lacks a tennis court." Principal Holly stood.

"One more question, Mr. Holly. Where were you this past Monday night between ten and eleven o'clock?"

"Home watching a documentary on whale migration. My wife and I have a trip to Iceland planned for early next month. You know, whales leave those waters in late October."

"No, I didn't know that." Steve clicked off his recorder and signaled Page.

Holly escorted them to the office door. "I understand you're planning to speak with Amos Park, the math department head?"

"Yes, he's on tap next. Why? Is there something you'd like to tell me about Mr. Park?"

"Just I heard some mumblings around the water cooler, so to say, that Amos was quite prickly a few days ago with Mr. Westin. I'm sure it was a matter of little importance, but I thought I should mention it."

"Thanks again, Mr. Holly. We'll be in touch should we

have more questions."

"Before you leave, have you any idea when I may expect Mr. Westin's return? It's challenging to find substitute teachers for short stints."

"I think you'll likely need someone to cover this school year. Bullet chest wounds can be nasty buggers. Thank you again." Steve nodded and stepped into the hall.

"A ghost teacher?" repeated Page. "I didn't get much from that whole exchange. I don't sense that Holly has anything to do with the murder. He's about as exciting as a monk baking bread. What about you?"

A grin appeared on Steve's face. "Nice image, but yes, same as you." Steve pointed to the corridor on the left.

Page stopped at the classroom signed Amos Park. "I always say, no harm in nosing."

Steve chuckled and opened the door. "And, that, Sherlocka, is how you and Betsy end up finding dead bodies. Nosey can get you hurt. After you."

Entering the classroom, the first thing that grabbed Page's attention was hastily scribbled math formulas on the chalkboard.

"Mr. Park, I'm Detective Tanner, and this police consultant, Page Wright. We're here, as you know, to chat about Dean Westin." Steve approached the teacher, who remained seated at his desk, wearing a scowling look.

"Strike one," Page muttered to herself.

"You have ten minutes before the students get to my class. If you want to sit, it'll be at a desk."

A surprised Page watched as Steve scooted two desks

around the side where Park sat. He was using intimidation early.

"Ms. Wright, please join me."

Park's reaction wasn't lost on Page. *Score one for the home team,* she thought.

"I'll get right to it, Park. If you haven't heard, Dean Westin was shot and is in the hospital."

"No, I had not heard this. How terrible for Mr. Westin."

Page gave a subtle grin. Steve wasn't lying. Dean was in the hospital morgue.

"I'm here to find out if you know anyone who'd like to unload a bullet into his chest. Why don't you start by telling me if you get along with him?" Steve turned sideways at the desk.

"Yes, mainly because he's complying with my department requirements and keeps a low profile, unlike some of my other teachers. So, yes, I'll say his early performance is satisfactory. As for who would want to shoot the man, who knows? We're not friends or anything. I make it a rule not to hang out with my teachers."

A redheaded siren stuck her head in the door, "Hey boss man, are we still on for a frolic later — oh sorry." The door closed.

"You were saying, Mr. Park, about not fraternizing with your staff?" Steve pressed.

An author couldn't have written a better scene. Page looked out the window to hide her mirth. Foolish man. She waited for Park's answer.

"My personal life is none of your business. You've got

less than five minutes to wrap this up."

"Let me explain the facts of life to you. First, I decide what my business is when it concerns an investigation. Second, you misrepresented — and that's me being generous in word choice — how you operate your department. Third, I've got as much time as I need with you in this classroom or down at the police interrogation room." Steve stood and bent over the teacher's desk to get eye to eye. "Fourth, and probably what you should pay most attention to, is that I don't think you and Dean get along."

"What? Who told you such nonsense? I resent — " Park's face turned red with anger.

Steve raised his hand. "To continue, I'm considering putting you on the suspect board. Trust me, finding yourself on my board is not a place you ever want to reside. Are you clear how things work in my investigations?"

Park shifted in his chair. "Yeah, clear, but you need to be clear on the fact that I had nothing to do with Westin getting shot."

"Then you won't mind telling me where you were the night Westin took a bullet."

"It might help if you told me when he took the bullet." Park watched two students enter and take their seats.

"This past Monday night between ten and eleven o'clock," Steve replied.

Page watched as the teacher pondered his answer.

"Monday night, I was home grading papers and watching football. I've answered your questions and now take off." Park motioned for a boy not to interrupt.

"How quickly you forget what I just told you. I'm not done yet. Can anyone corroborate your story?" asked Steve.

"Yeah, my wife, but don't bother her with this nonsense. Time for you two to go. I've got a class to teach. Nice meeting you. Tell Dean I'll try to get by to see him in a few days. He owes me a monthly student assessment." Park walked to the front of the class with papers to hand out.

"Aw, Mr. Park, don't give us another pop quiz," said a tall teenage boy sitting in the back.

"Quit moaning, you stupid jock."

Steve nodded to Page.

They walked to his SUV in silence. Neither had anything to add to the two interviews. Page decided to stay quiet about the unusual calculations on the blackboard in Park's class. She turned her focus to the dark clouds rolling over Shell Isle.

"Looks tropical up there." Steve pointed to the sky. "The storm must have sped up. We're supposed to get a Cat 2 blow."

"Yeah, I kept hoping it would veer west. I noticed the chop on the water this morning, and the lifeguard put out the 'no swimming' sign despite the sunshine. Our weather has definitely become weird and unpredictable. Ask the penguins and polar bears." Page sighed and climbed into the vehicle.

Steve drove out of the parking lot. "I'm happy to help with preps at Hibiscus."

"Really?" Page smiled.

"Yep. Really. Let me guess. You need the hurricane shutters secured."

Page nodded, and her mouth turned up at the corners. "I'll help and feed you."

"Okay, but on one condition. You feed me something prepared by you and not the Firestarter Betsy. Agreed?" Steve extended his arm across the console.

Page shook his hand and leaned over to hug him. "Thank you, Steve. I've got plenty of candles if you need some."

"Nope, I plan to stay at your place during the storm."

"My place? Why my place?" Page frowned.

"Because you've made friends with two uninvited suspects, and I'm not going to ask an officer to remain in his vehicle during a hurricane watching your cottage."

"No, of course not. I doubt anyone would make mischief—"

"It's the ideal time to make trouble. Besides, I'm looking forward to trying some new body contortions on that wicker thing you call a sofa. Though I swear, I picked three splinters from my calves this morning."

"Why would you get splinters on your—?"

"Because I had to hang my damn legs off the sofa's back. That's why."

Page erupted into laughter and then hiccupped.

"I don't see the humor here. Can we not talk about this anymore?" Steve's cell phone rang.

Page glanced out the window, holding the vision of Steve looking like a pretzel on Aunt Tilly's settee.

"Great! Finally, a break in this case. Yep, set it up." Steve tossed his phone in the cup holder. "We got Knuckles."

CHAPTER 13

"Fantastic! One down and three motley types to go. Validating Park's alibi will determine his fate on my suspect board. What's next?" Page sensed the pace of gathering clues would amp up.

"Next, I either drop you at Honey Bees or suffer Betsy's wrath. Andre will spend the rest of the morning with you two until his replacement shows up. Koch is in charge of providing protection, so I can't tell you who drew the next short straw." Steve pulled in front of the shop.

"Short straw? That little remark is going to cost you, buster," threatened Page. "Just for the short straw wise crack, I've decided to keep a certain earlier observation to myself." Page lifted the door handle.

Steve reached for Page's free arm. "Hey, I was joking. I need to know what you're holding back...again."

"You were not joking, Detective Tanner." Page tried to get out, but Steve held on. She hid her amusement.

"Mostly, I was kidding. Tell me. Please," cajoled Steve.

"Nope. I'm going to ponder it first. I'll see you later to button up my shutters. Ta, ta."

"Ta, ta yourself, Page Wright. You'll hear from me sooner than you think." Steve hollered through the open SUV's window.

Page marched into Honey Bees, passed a seated Andre, waved to Daisy, ringing up a customer, and found Betsy in the kitchen with Ina. "I'm here."

"Obviously." Betsy handed Ina two clean mixer blades. "Beat that pumpkin cookie batter with extra love, Ina. I promised Andre a freshly baked one." Betsy re-tied her apron and came to Page. "What's up?"

Page motioned for Betsy to follow her to the storeroom. "I didn't want to talk about the case in front of Ina."

"Hurry and spill it, sista. I have pumpkin walnut cupcakes waiting for their frosting."

"Fine. Here's your condensed morning update. We went to the high school and met with the principal and the math department head. I saw Knuckles driving down the side street by the school parking lot."

"Whoa there. A Knuckles sighting is good." Betsy closed the door.

"Yep. Steve called in the vehicle, and an officer nabbed him lickety-split. I expect questioning will happen soon. No one seems to care or know much about Dean. Amos, the math head, wasn't cooperative and showed plenty of attitude at being bothered. Steve took him down a few pegs." Page's eyes danced, recalling.

"Detective Dreamboat excels at take-downs. What about alibis?" Betsy grabbed a bottled tea from a shelf.

Page's face showed surprise.

"Don't give me that look. I know the drill. Alibi?"

"Amos has an alibi for the night Dean was killed. Of course, Steve has to verify it."

"Did the principal have an alibi?" Betsy pressed the bottle to her cheek. "Flash incoming."

"Principal Holly was home with his wife watching some documentary on whales. I doubt he's involved. Total milquetoast type."

Betsy nodded. "I dated a guy once. I think his name was Mitchell, who I'd describe as milque—"

"Forget Mitchell. While I was at Steve's, I discovered another cipher in the morning paper's classifieds. I'll write it down for you. We need to figure this out, Betsy, like yesterday. We know there's another meeting for Dean, but not when." Page grabbed a paper and pen. "Here you go. Also, when I was in Amos's classroom, I noticed some complex math formulas on the chalkboard."

"So what? He teaches math, Page. You're trying to make something out of nothing here. Remember, math isn't your strong suit, so complex to you is probably high school calculus."

"Yeah, you're probably right." Page straightened cans of pumpkin lining the shelves. She chose to ignore counting how many cases of pumpkin purée were stacked in a corner. That math she could do.

"Moving along, we know the case is wrapped around ciphering and ciphers." Betsy paused. "What's a cipher anyway?"

"It's some super-secret code using mathematical algorithms. If a person can crack the cipher, they've got the entrance into the code...I think."

"I'm sorry I asked. And I'm even more sorry you

landed us a case needing an IQ of two hundred to solve. Other than the big nab of Knuckles, the high school visit sounds like a dead-end for clues or any real suspect." Betsy tossed the empty tea bottle in the trash. "Listen, I need to get back to my cupcakes. Those I understand."

Page chuckled. "Go frost them. I've got some boxes of lavender honey body cream to unpack and put out. Plus, Daisy needs help assembling the new carousel display of honey lip balm. We'll have time to chat more tonight. The storm's coming our way."

"Geez, we've got to wrestle those shutters —"

"Nope. Steve's earning his keep tonight and going to handle the task."

"I haven't had a moment to plan dinner. I can whip up a Mex Meatloaf with poblanos and —"

Page panicked and jumped in. "Don't worry about dinner. We'll order pizzas. I'm hoping we can resurrect our trusty suspect board before Steve shows. It's time we plot these suspects."

Ina's voice rang out. "Betsy, I need you! You've got three timers going off."

~*~

By late afternoon, Honey Bees was humming along. The baked goods were replenished for the last-minute customers, and Daisy had the body care displays fully stocked and dusted. Andre had become the sampler and was parked in the kitchen. Page slipped behind the silk screen to hang her apron when the door's bell jingled.

"Welcome to Honey Bees. Is there something special

you'd like from the cookie trays?" asked Daisy.

"I need a couple of dozen cookies for a teacher meeting. Choose any varieties. I don't care, but make it snappy," said a gruff male voice.

"Sure. Give me a sec, and I'll box them for you."

Page heard a cell phone ring. The man's footsteps drew closer to her.

"Where the hell have you been? I don't care about your latest meditation retreat. Never mind; listen to me carefully. If the police stop by—I said, listen, Ellen. If the police stop by, make sure you tell them I was home with you Monday evening."

Page stood in shock. Amos Park was standing a few feet away and blowing his alibi to Key West.

"Don't screw this up, or you'll be meditating on a cushion in front of the television screen and not some posh place in Tibet." Park ended the call.

Page looked through the screen's slats and saw him at the counter paying Daisy. She waited for the sound of the door closing before stepping out. The cell phone in her pocket chimed. Page released a held breath. Good thing the incoming call waited for Park to depart. "Hey, Steve. You won't believe—now? You're outside?" Page hurried to the entrance.

"Yeah, I see you. Give me a minute to tell Betsy."

Betsy materialized. "Where are you going? I thought we—"

"I gotta dash. Steve's waiting to take me to the station. Don't forget I'll bring the pizzas home later." Page pivoted.

"FYI, Amos Park just left with a bag of cookies and a parting gift for us."

"A parting gift?" Betsy glanced around.

"I heard Amos ask his wife to lie and cover his alibi. See ya later, kiddo."

CHAPTER 14

A breathless Page pulled the passenger door closed in Steve's vehicle. "Whew! Let's go. I didn't expect to see your mug again this soon, but I do appreciate the unexpected invite to Knuckles' questioning."

"Oh, I'm buttering you up for tonight." Steve winked.

"A complete waste of effort with my duenna taking up space at Hibiscus. So much space." Page clipped her hair back and offered a 'poor me' face.

"Actually, I was referring to your handling of dinner, so I don't have to eat Betsy's fare." Steve offered Page a mint and another wink.

Page felt her face color. "Oh." She accepted the peppermint, giving her time to think of a comeback. "Well, I'm happy to report your buttering is for naught. Dinner is takeout pizza. Moving on. What do you have planned for Knuckles?"

Steve's mouth thinned. "You know, Page, this is one of those times I've got practically nil on a suspect. It's going to be tricky to get him talking. He's waiting for me in the interview room, but I need you observing and inkling."

"Tanner, I don't inkle. I get inklings. I guess I should feel grateful you didn't call them 'tinklings,' as in I need you tinkling." Page rolled her eyes.

"Funny, but can you please be serious?"

The peppermint triggered a sneeze and an inkling. Page looked heavenward through the moonroof and mouthed, "Thank you."

Steve handed her a tissue. "Look, I'm a detective with a stumper of a case, with no one visiting my pretend Dean in the hospital, and with a lowlife suspect not cooperating. Right now, all my file has is three lousy encrypted pages." Steve pulled into his reserved spot in the police parking lot.

Page leaned across the console and patted Steve's cheek. "Add to the list that you're a detective having to depend on a 'snoop' for assistance. Lead the way. I plan to save your day."

~*~

Sitting in the observation room with one-way glass, Page took a moment to study Knuckle's demeanor and appearance. He wore the sinister air well. She noticed his mouth held a permanent snarl, and his bulbous nose had taken a fist more than once. Page felt a shiver when Knuckles stared at the glass. She knew he couldn't see her, but something in his eyes unnerved her. They were dead and without emotion.

Both detectives entered the room. Steve took a seat across from Knuckles. Koch leaned against the door as a deterrent to the suspect leaving without a blessing. "Let's get started." Steve flipped on the recorder switch. "You've been Mirandized and have waived attorney representation. Is that correct?"

"Correct."

"State your full name."

"Antonio Luigi Furazio, but I prefer Tony."

"Sounds like a pasta entrée to me," Koch interjected.

A laugh escaped Page. "Now I have your real name." She grabbed the legal pad from the table and wrote it down.

"The address where you reside, Mr. Furazio?" Steve's voice remained monotone.

"I'd rather not provide that information." Tony tugged on his shirt's collar.

"This wise guy's moves are straight from a mobster movie." Page glanced out the door to make sure no one heard her.

"Really? You're being uncooperative on question two? Not a good plan, Tony. Maybe you want to rethink this."

Page nodded. Steve was using Tony's first name to chill him down. Would it work?

"Okay, let me say it in general terms. I live in the area of Chapel, New Jersey. What else yous wanna know? I've got a large pie ordered from Vinny's Pizzeria to pick up in—" Tony glanced at his watch. "In about thirty."

"So, Tony from Chapel, Jersey, let's talk about why you're in Shell Isle." Steve waited.

"Yeah, well, I'm sort of vacationing. Came to see my pal, Dean."

"You must know your pal Dean is in the nearby hospital recovering from a bullet that came too close to his ticker."

"No kiddin? I was planning to stop by his place with the pizza and see if he wanted to go fishing later." Tony tried and failed to cross his leg.

"Your answer confuses me. Want to know why?" Steve sat back in his chair.

"Educate me, Detective —" Tony squinted at Steve's badge. "Tanner."

"It's quite simple. Dean is a teacher. School is in session. He wouldn't be home until late afternoon."

Koch chuckled. "Mr. Furazio, your story has what I call a flat tire. Why don't you save us all time here and shoot straight? Sorry, wrong choice of words."

"Slipped my mind about Dean teaching today. Like I said, I'm on vacation." Tony spied the water pitcher on a nearby table. "I could use a drink."

Koch poured him a glass of water.

"Nice little beach town yous got here. Haven't found the locals too friendly. Yeah, I'm planning to cut out in a day or so and head down the coast Miami way. I've got some business there. Dean's too busy to party."

"I bet Dean would like a visit, Tony." Steve paused and looked at his notes. "To continue, we're trying to find out who shot Dean. While we may not be friendly, we're known for our fine accommodations inside the jail. Koch has quite a knack for pairing up roommates."

"Thanks, Steve. I've got a guy in cell four that I think Tony will connect with. He's from Jersey, too. About six foot, five inches and a bit rough around the edges. He keeps flashing pictures of himself as a prize fighter. I'm happy to introduce you, Tony, if you don't want to answer our questions." Koch leaned against the door.

"Enough of your wisecracks. What else do you want to know?" Tony finished his water.

Steve sat next to Tony. "Where were you last Monday

night between the hours of ten and eleven o'clock?"

"Hmm." Tony stroked his double chin. "That's the night I picked up a lady of the evening. We spent a few hours getting to know each other pretty well. She left my motel room around midnight."

"Did your lady have a name?" asked Steve.

"She called herself Velvet," Tony smirked. "And I can attest—"

"Velvet? You've got to be kidding me." Koch looked at Steve. "Know any of the street gals called Velvet?"

"Nope," Steve added a few notes to his tablet.

Tony stood with his self-confidence. "Let me help you figure some things out. It doesn't make sense that I'd try to kill my pal. Yous need to keep looking. I ain't your man. Guess we're done here."

"Sit down. I say when we're done. When's the last time you saw your pal, Dean?"

"That would be Monday morning before he went to school. I met him for coffee at some local joint in town. Lousiest cup of coffee I ever tasted." Tony made a face.

"Yes, a couple of witnesses placed you at The Perk."

Tony's face showed surprise. "Small town gossips, no doubt. We done? My pie—"

"One more question before I take you for a short ride. You were seen exchanging laptops with Dean. I'd like to know the reason." Steve waited.

Page sensed Tony was conjuring up an explanation. She got an inkling along with a question for Steve. She went to the door and motioned to the officer behind the front desk.

"Yes, ma'am? What do you need?"

"Could you please interrupt Detective Tanner and ask him to step into the observation room for a moment?" Page hustled back.

Steve poked his head in the room. "Tell me you've got something. I've got a flame out with this guy."

"I got an inkling. Shake up Tony by saying he was seen going into Dean's condo around midnight. I assume the police hadn't gone there yet. You're looking for the answer to what Dean had that Tony wanted?"

"Thanks, Page. Those inklings are—"

"And, don't you forget it, buster. Now, go crush it."

Page watched Steve pour Tony another glass of water. "Here you go. So, back to the laptop exchange. Have you come up with something other than the truth?"

"Hey, I've been nothing but honest. Dean knows computers. Mine was acting up, so he loaned me one of his while he ran...what do you call it?" Tony stared off. "A scan? He found some things and fixed them. Nothing more to it."

"What do you think, Tanner?" asked Koch.

"I think there's more to this laptop story. Tony, I'm going to ask you to turn the machine over to us. You'll get it back when our IT guys finish having their way with it."

"Look, man. I can't let you have the computer. It's got private things—"

"We don't care if you're into porn." Koch tossed out.

Tony rubbed the sweat from his forehead. "It's a business computer. Okay? There's confidential information—"

"Okay, let's put this subject on hold. I have another

pressing question." Steve signaled Koch to return to the door.

Page understood the maneuver. He was afraid Tony was close to bolting.

"You were seen leaving Dean's condo around midnight on the night he was murdered. Want to tell us why you were there? What did you take?"

"I wasn't at Dean's. I was with Velvet."

"Your pie is getting cold. Answer the questions." Steve's voice sounded impatient.

"Or I can activate your room reservation, Tony," supplied Koch.

"So, okay, I stopped by Dean's after me and Velvet parted ways. He wasn't there."

"You went inside his unit. Did you pick the lock?" asked Steve.

"I don't pick anything but my teeth. The knob needed a quick jiggle, is all. Big deal." Tony looked toward the door.

"That jiggle is called breaking and entering. I'll make a note of the charge." Koch nodded. "I think our Tony is about to add theft to our list. Aren't you Tony?"

"You're reachin' man. Dean's my pal. I was looking for what was mine. That's not stealing."

"Exactly what was yours? Tony, I'm getting tired of pulling your teeth one by one. Right now, I feel the temptation to break your jaw."

"It was no big deal. Dean had lifted a couple of fake driver's licenses and birth certificates from my motel room. I'd found the lot and wanted them back to destroy. I know it's illegal to possess fake documents."

"What an outstanding citizen we have here, Steve."

Page shook her head. Tony was a big liar.

Steve returned to Page. "He's not going to spill tonight. I don't want to arrest him...yet. I need someone to show up at the hospital. Plus, I've got to request a warrant to get my hands on that laptop. You got anything else?"

"Nope. The jerk's holding out. His back isn't against the wall, and he knows it. My worry is Tony taking off for Miami, where you'll never find him."

"I can take care of the concern by keeping him under surveillance. I'd planned to." Steve turned to leave.

"Don't forget the hurricane is coming. Tony will want to get out of Shell tonight."

"Not going to happen. I'll figure out how to keep the officer watching him safely. We'll put a monitor on Tony's door."

Page nodded. "That should do the trick."

"I've got one more chain to pull before I turn Tony loose. Then, we'll head to Vinnie's for the pizzas to bring home. I'll lay you odds Vinnie won't have a pie waiting on our pal Tony." Steve smiled and disappeared.

"So, Tony, it's getting late, and your takeout order is waiting. Here's the way things go for you. First, you're not to leave Shell Isle. Second, I will get a warrant since you don't want to hand over the laptop. Koch and I will decide what we're going to charge you with while you reconsider talking to us." Steve waited for a few beats while Tony fidgeted in the chair. "I saved the best for last. To show you I'm a nice guy, I want to personally drive you to see your good pal, Dean. Let's see if he can corroborate the yarn you spun."

Tony jumped up. "Hell, no. I'm not going to the hospital to see Dean." Tony flapped his arms in the air like a bird ready to take flight. "I get all haywire around doctors and hospitals and those dangling bags with needles." Tony's eyes looked wild. "I've got what you call PSDT. Besides, Dean may not remember things right, being all drugged up. Hell no."

"What in the Sam Hill is PSDT? Is it catching?" Koch backed away.

"I think Tony means PTSD. I seriously doubt this clown suffers from it. I think it's more likely he causes it," answered Steve.

"Come on, princess, let's get your evening planned out." Koch hoisted Knuckles out of the chair and toward the door.

Page doubled over, laughing at the scene. Too bad the dialogue couldn't find its way into a movie. Tony was unraveling emotionally. She understood Steve's MO. A visit to the hospital was never a reality. It was meant as a shakeup. Steve planned to leave Tony in this high anxiety state overnight and see what panic stunt he might pull.

Steve appeared in the observation room's doorway.

"Well done, Detective Tanner." Page grabbed her handbag and joined Steve.

"Why, thank you kindly, ma'am." Steve tipped his black ball cap. "Ready for Vinnie's pizza?"

"Yep. I texted Betsy and got her pizza order." Page gave a little shrug.

Walking down the hallway with Page, Steve nodded at two officers, giving them a thumbs up. "Those guys are Tony's babysitters."

"Ah, you went for two officers instead of one. Smart. Tony's wily even with PSDT." Laughter claimed Page once again.

"What a stooge," said a laughing Steve. They exited the building. "Operation Flush is overdue for results. Our murderer needs a hefty dose of impatience. It's time for someone to kill Dean a second time."

"How about this, detective? I've got a juicy tidbit I've been holding for you."

Steve halted at the SUV's passenger door. "Hang on. I thought we understood each other. You're not to hold back tidbits as you call them because—"

Hands on her hips, Page fired back. "You hang on. I was getting ready to tell you when you called from outside Honey Bees. You were in a rush to get to Tony's party. I knew it could wait. Do you want to stand here wasting time, or do you want to hear?"

"Fine. You're right. Lay it on me, Sherlocka."

Page waited a moment to reply.

"What now?" Steve's tone sounded weary.

"Nothing. I'm taking a sec to savor being told I'm right. Those are two rare words coming from your lips." Page reached for the door handle. "Amos Park's alibi is fabricated. Yep, he told us a whopper. Expect his wife to lie for him."

CHAPTER 15

The sky had turned different shades of grey, sending the sun into hiding. Sunset was a no-show. Instead, evening delivered the coming storm's warning to prepare and hunker down. The wind had garnered speed as the first rain bands pelted Steve's windshield. A voice from the police radio asked all emergency responders to report to work.

Page unclasped her hands to release worry. "Does it mean you need to go back to the station tonight?"

Steve shook his head. "Not at this point. I don't think the hurricane's predicted to cause serious damage other than local flooding and power outages. In my experience, the thugs stay home until after a storm. As far as Dean's investigation, Koch and I have the officers in position with instructions. We're both on alert."

"It sounds like you've buttoned what you can." Page breathed in the pizza aroma lofting from the backseat. "Vinnie sure busted Tony's story about having a carryout pizza order. The big liar."

Steve nodded. "Tony's fast at spinning lies up. Look, the fog is getting soupy."

"Thankfully, here's Hibiscus." Page frowned. "I wonder whose vehicle is parked in my driveway? I assumed Ina would give Betsy a ride home, and the officer assigned would park elsewhere."

Steve pulled in his bungalow's drive. "We're about to find out. Let me grab Barn first. He's probably chewed every leg off my tables, waiting to get fed. Humor me and stay in the car. I don't want you entering the cottage alone."

"I'm sitting tight. Bring an umbrella back with you. I melt easily."

Steve pulled Page into him and kissed her. "Yes, you do. Fact is, I'd like to—"

"Stop it." Page enjoyed their bantering and the kissing even more. "Your timing is lousy. I'm starving, and the pizzas are getting cold. Hup to and get that pooch."

Moments later, Steve tapped on the glass, motioning for Page. An open umbrella in one hand and Barnacle attached to a leash in the other, he waited for her to exit. "I'll grab the pizzas if you can take Barn."

"Yep. Hey, Barnacle. Food's coming, and I've got a bone I saved for you." Page stayed close to Steve as they ran to the porch.

"Hang on a sec. Before we go in, I want to check something." Steve jogged down the sidewalk to the parked vehicle and shone his flashlight inside. Wearing an impish grin, he returned. "All clear. Let's eat."

Page entered the cottage. Surprise came calling, along with a crack of lightning.

"Finally, you show up. We're past starving and ready to eat cardboard." Betsy relieved Steve of the pizza boxes.

Andre placed the last napkin on the dining table and waved. "Evening, Page and Steve. I hope you don't mind me joining, but Betsy insisted—"

"Of course, they don't mind you dining with us. Everyone, take a seat. Barnacle, I've got your bowl over in the corner." Betsy deposited the pizza boxes on the table. "Page, close your yap and claim a pie."

Plastering a pleasant expression on her face, Page sat. "Andre, we're happy you're here."

"Thank you. I haven't made many friends yet, so I'm grateful."

Steve acted first and lifted the lid. "Yeah, Andre recently joined the force. He's proven an asset from day one."

"Thanks, Steve." Andre tucked the napkin under his chin.

Betsy peered into the open box. "Who ordered peppers and black olives?"

"Me." Page placed the box on her placemat next to a glass of unknown liquid brewed by Betsy.

"I've got a pizza with spinach, pineapple, cheddar, ham, and some kind of hot—That's gotta be—"

"Mine." Betsy reached for her box.

"I've got a French influence going with bleu cheese, bacon, and mushrooms. By process of elimination, here you go, Andre." Page recognized Betsy had found a kindred spirit.

"The last is the boring pepperoni, which I proudly claim." Steve pulled a large slice out of the box and closed the lid. "Can't go wrong with pep. What's the blue liquid in the glass?"

"It's an infusion of blueberry and green tea with a splash of ginger to help digestion. There's a big pitcher in the fridge, so don't be shy, as I like to say."

Page took a sip and coughed. "Pardon me. The ginger made a big splash in my glass."

Andre and Steve exchanged worried looks before sampling.

"C'est bon," Andre nodded to Betsy.

"Of course, it's bon. I make everything bon." Betsy fluffed her hair and grabbed a second slice. She proceeded to sprinkle red pepper flakes atop.

This time, it was Steve who coughed.

Betsy fired a warning flare look toward Steve. "Why don't you update us on Dean's case?"

After sharing the latest case news, Page shifted the conversation to a new topic. "Andre, I'd love to hear how you came to Shell Isle."

"Ah, yes." Andre nodded. "There were three reasons that sent me south. First, I'd lost my work partner on a bust, and my heart partner decided she wanted to work on a cruise ship. Third, the Canadian winters were challenging now that I'm older. So, I remembered vacationing at Shell Isle and how it offered warmer climes and a low crime rate. I made the move, and, fortunately, Detectives Koch and Tanner hired me. Now, my only regret is waiting so long." Andre's expression warmed as he glanced at Betsy.

"Shell Isle is like no other beach town. You chose well, Andre, and it's great to have you here," said Page. She heard Barnacle gnawing on his bone. At least he was on a towel and not her hibiscus area rug.

"Thanks, Page." Andre scooted his chair back and

looked at everyone. "I'd like to hear all of your Shell Isle stories."

They went around the table, telling how Shell Isle called to them.

The four ignored the sound of the wind's howl growing louder. They enjoyed an easy camaraderie and lingered at the table long after removing the pizza boxes.

~*~

"My apologies to each of you." Andre stood first. "It's past nine o'clock. I need to go before the weather deteriorates further." He went to the window. "I see a few small limbs are already down."

"Uh oh. The lights just flickered. Too bad no one has a generator." Betsy pulled her fan from her pocket. "I need air conditioning twenty-four-seven, and this fan ain't it."

Steve reached for his cell phone. "I'll check for the latest hurricane — not good news here."

"What's not good news? My shutters aren't even up." Page leaned over, trying to see the phone screen.

"Tanner, lay it on us." Betsy headed to the refrigerator.

"It's still hanging on as a category two storm, and it's moving faster. Looks like Shell Isle will get some action." Steve tossed his phone on the table. "I'd better get the shutters up on both our homes without delay. They can't wait."

"Listen, Steve, I can stay and give you a hand with them. I've never been in a hurricane prep zone, but I'm a fast learner." Andre stepped away from the window.

"Gosh, you guys are our knights in shining armor. Aren't they, Page?" Betsy peered inside the refrigerator, moving things around.

"Yes, they are knights. I'm so appreciative of the help. I don't possess enough brawn for those heavy things. Andre, are you sure it's safe for you to delay leaving?"

Betsy set what looked like a cream pie on the island with a flourish. "I'm sure Andre is capable of taking care of himself. French Canadian men are, you know."

"Your cousin is correct. Please, don't give it another thought. I'm going to need a rain check on the pie." Andre gave a wry smile.

"Raincheck for me, too, Betsy." Steve nodded.

"Rainchecks all around. Can do." Betsy slid the pie back inside the refrigerator.

"Anytime you're ready, Steve. I'm going to the vehicle to get my rain slicker. See you outside." Andre opened the door. A gust of wind blew it against the wall, making a loud thud. "All fine here. Don't worry."

"Ladies, you might want to gather the candles and flashlights. Fill the tub with water. You know the drill." Steve hesitated. "Betsy, do you need us to button up your bungalow?"

"Aw, Steve, how nice of you. My contractor had his crew secure the place this morning. Hurry back for my pie. It's my thank you."

"You're too good to me, Ms. Ross. I don't deserve—"

Page interjected. "Oh, yes, you do. You deserve two ginormous slices of this…"

"Rarin' Rhubarb Cream Pie," said Betsy. "It's the new name I gave the original boring recipe. It called for dark chocolate and strawberries. My version is so much tastier, especially if you add butterscotch sauce and a smidge of cardamom." Betsy glanced in Steve's direction.

Page covered her mouth, amused at the shade of green Steve had turned. "Yep, we'll have two big slices waiting on you, big boy. I'll even cut them myself."

Steve bolted out the door.

"So much for getting the suspect board out tonight. Let's get prepared while we have power." Page reached for three empty pitchers and flicked the faucet lever.

Betsy moved toward the bathroom. "I'll take tub and candle duty. I've got a load of wet clothes I'd better put in the dryer while we have power to —"

The cottage went dark.

CHAPTER 16

Steve opened the cottage's front door. "Listen up, the power is out in our area. We saw the transformer blow when a live oak clipped it. And the street's already blocked."

Page came to the foyer. "Do you think the power company will attempt to get it repaired?" She noticed the water streaming down Steve's face and resisted the urge to wipe it away.

"Doubtful. They'll need a bucket truck, and I don't think these wind gusts will allow the guys to go up. At least, your shutters were easy to attach. We'll head to my place next. Stay inside."

"Hang on, handsome." Page hurried to grab a towel.

"I like it when you call me names. It's a turn on and—"

"No hanky-panky," hollered Betsy from another room.

Page reappeared. "You heard my duenna. Here, you're soaked." She tossed him a towel. "Be careful out there, okay?"

Steve delivered a smart salute. "I'm more worried about eating the pie in your fridge than I am about some rain and wind." He closed the door.

He wasn't alone with the worry. Page took the flashlight and went to find the perpetrator of her digestive woes. "Hey, you found candles, and the tub is full." Page patted Betsy's back.

Barnacle came to investigate. Getting ignored, he returned to his corner in the living room.

"Yep, I've got wet clothes in the washer next on my list. I gotta find a place to hang them." Betsy swiped her brow. "Without air conditioning, I'm in for the longest hot flash in history. A miserable night of frizzy hair, my night gown will cling to me like plastic wrap to a bowl of—well, you get the idea. At least it's just you and me tonight. I can look like a wet dishrag without witnesses." Betsy turned off her flashlight and lit a candle.

"Uhm, Bets, about us being alone, Steve is planning—"

"Are you about to tell me Dreamboat is spending another night in the living room? I can't move about in my night gown if he's hanging off Aunt Tilly's sofa." Betsy grabbed a breath.

"We'll figure something out. And this is the place where I say, 'please notice I haven't grilled you about your potential new dreamboat dining with us.'"

"After my red lipstick failed to attract anyone's interest at the bowling alley, I needed a little lift. Hang on, trickster. Andre's guarding us for pity's sake, though he does possess a certain—"

"Yep, I knew your wandering eye was active again. Didn't take you long." Page teased. "Still, we need Steve's presence here. These five suspects aren't nice people. Not one of them." Page held up her fingers.

"I'm not worried. Dean's friends aren't coming to mess with us in the middle of a hurricane. Where is Detective Dreamboat? I heard his voice a minute ago. We need to have a chat about his accommodations."

"He went outside to finish the shutters. Come on, Bets. Let's show Steve some gratitude for a change and not some lip. Go deal with your wet frocks while I chase down my portable phone charger. That's one gadget I'm glad you talked me into purchasing." Page needed to elevate Betsy's mood.

"One day, you'll learn Betsy knows best." Betsy turned around. "Where did you go?"

~*~

"I hope you don't mind that I draped my wet slicker across the porch railing to dry and left my shoes at the door." Andre stood on the porch next to Steve.

"I don't mind at all, and thank you again, Andre." Page stretched a beckoning hand inside.

Steve dropped his wet boots and wiped his hands on the towel Page had given him earlier. He draped his poncho over the porch swing. "We finished getting the shutters up. I've shut everything off at my bungalow."

"That's good. You won't need to worry about things," said Page. She watched as the men shook the umbrellas free of water. The blowing rain stung her face. She stepped away from the door.

Steve entered the foyer and laid his overnight satchel on the rattan chair. "It's getting worse out there. Another tree is across the road out front. I'm afraid Andre is stuck here until the cleanup tomorrow."

"I don't want to cause an imposition on you nice ladies. I can sleep in my vehicle." Andre bent to unroll the cuffs of his jeans.

"Not another word, Andre. You will stay with us at Hibiscus," answered Page.

"That's settled. Any chance of getting something hot to drink that's prepared by you?" asked Steve.

"Since we have a gas cooktop, the answer is yes. Coffee or tea?" Page led the way to the kitchen and filled a tea kettle.

"Black coffee extra strong for me." Steve perched on the bar stool.

"I'm with him. Make it a double," said Andre.

Betsy appeared with hangers dangling seven wet Mumus. "I'm going to hang these around the cottage to dry." Seeing Andre, her face reddened. "On second thought." Betsy pivoted and disappeared.

Page smiled at the two men. "She'll be back in a second."

"Can you hurry that instant coffee?" Steve's eyes darted toward Betsy's room.

"If you'll take it lukewarm, then yes." Page dropped a heaping teaspoon of granules into the mugs.

"Just do it. Betsy's singing. That doesn't bode well for us. That's when she gets her creative ideas." Steve's voice was laced with concern.

"And, you know this *how*?" Page's eyebrow lifted.

"She told me once. These things I remember. Pour already." Steve reached for the closest mug.

"You both seem mighty ruffled over Betsy's kitchen involvement." Andre's expression went from amused to serious when he saw the Mumu moving their way.

"Tempt fate if you dare," cautioned Page.

"Better slide my tepid coffee over." Andre reached for the sugar bowl.

"I'm back. What did I miss? Oh, coffee." Betsy peered into the three cups. "Looks boring. Let me jazz it up for you." She grabbed a jar of nutmeg.

"We're good here. Why don't we move to the living room where there's more candlelight? Page claimed her favorite comfy chair. She waited until everyone found a place. "Steve, can you check for weather updates? The wind sounds stronger."

Barnacle gave a whine, joined the group, and curled up next to Steve's feet. His eyes remained alert.

"That's an omen." Betsy pointed at the dog. "He's not chewing a bone. Barn always chews something."

"He's a good dog." Andre bent over and patted Barnacle's head.

"The latest is better news. It's back to a category one storm. It'll come in at low tide, so that's good, too. By mid-morning tomorrow, other than cleanup, things should return to normal." Steve placed his cell phone on the end table and sipped his cold coffee.

"Well, what a relief. Maybe we can open Honey Bees in the afternoon." Betsy delivered a smile Andre's way. "I'm making pumpkin almond scones with a dash of —"

"Love," interjected Page. "I've got it. Why don't we use the time to try to crack the classified code?"

"Remind me what it is, please." Steve grabbed the tablet and pen from the table.

"0925-2100CS," Page watched as Steve wrote. "I

confess that I'm lousy with numbers."

Betsy's face brightened. "Listen to my terrific idea. Why don't we split into teams and work on it? The winners get one of my scrumptious frozen ginger cupcakes. Andre, want to partner?" Betsy waited.

"It would be my pleasure," said Andre.

"I'm in." Steve nodded to Page.

"Me, too. I can vouch for those cupcakes being scrumptious."

Andre rose and extended his hand to Betsy. "Mademoiselle, shall we?"

A flustered Betsy accepted his hand and moved them to the dining table.

~*~

The evening gave way to the wee hours. Shell Isle accepted the wind and rain lashing with the same resilience as its residents. Hibiscus Cottage's lights flickered before rewarding the four with a lit room. No one could sleep with the wind waking every creak in the house. The group worked to solve the code between cups of Betsy's 'fortified' hot cocoa and punchy teasing amongst the couples.

Page and Steve disappeared into her study around two in the morning, claiming they couldn't concentrate with Betsy's mumbling numbers. They left Andre agreeing to a slice of Betsy's pie.

~*~

Andre rubbed his forehead. "I think we should take a break. Maybe something will come to us later."

"I agree. It's all a jumble to me. I know. Why don't I

pick a mystery movie for us?" Betsy grabbed the remote and moved to the sofa. "Coming?"

"Yes, yes, of course." Andre offered a slight smile. "What's the flick?"

"The Capon Mystery Series. You're going to love these two sleuths." Betsy pointed to the screen.

"I'm sure I will." Andre settled back.

"See them in the bistro's kitchen? They specialize in capon entrees, thus the name, Capon Mysteries."

"I see." Andre watched Betsy and not the television.

"I always tell Page that she and I should have a television series. We're far more interesting and exceptional with our sleuthing than—"

"I quite agree." Andre's eyes remained on Betsy.

"You do?" Betsy caught her breath. Her full attention shifted to the man sitting next to her.

"Oh, yes. I see you are an exceptional woman in every way, Mademoiselle Ross."

"I am?" Betsy answered, her voice a bit breathless.

"Most definitely." Andre turned to the screen. "Ah, these women look most dedicated to seasoning the capon with proper French herbs. I appreciate a chef knowing how to blend herbs and spices."

"I need my fan." Betsy reached for her handbag sitting on the coffee table. "I may need a fan for each hand."

~*~

"I can't believe you figured out whodunit just as the movie ended and we lost power again," said Betsy, switching off the television.

"You forget I've been in law enforcement for many decades. Your deducing skills were impressive. You simply took a small wrong turn otherwise—"

"Yes, otherwise, I would have guessed correctly." Betsy bobbed her head.

"Exactly. Shall we try cracking the cipher again?"

~*~

"By golly, Miss Molly, we've almost solved it. Page, come out here and see what you think." Betsy looked at Andre. "Silence means hanky panky with those two."

Andre released a chuckle. "Want me to investigate?"

"Better you than me. Go for it." Betsy stared down at the two letters at the end of the entry.

An amused Andre returned. "They fell asleep. I stole a peek at what was written on the notepad."

"And?" whispered Betsy.

"Let me say it like this. We have no competition. I see one of your famous ginger cupcakes in my future."

"I like you, Andre Lyon." Betsy tucked more frizz behind her ear.

"In that case, would you consider dining with me at a place I keep hearing is a must-go?" Andre sat down. His cobalt blue eyes fixed on Betsy.

"Since I'm out of male purgatory, I say yes, of course."

"Male purgatory?" Andre's expression changed from pleased to confused. "I struggle with American English."

"Never mind. It's Page's twisted method of displaying way too much concern over my social life. Tell me the place where we're dining." Betsy batted her lashes and activated her dormant flirting technique.

"Yes, well, it's called the Crab Shak."

Betsy's face lit up. "The Crab Shak. Oh my gosh! That's it, Andre." She wrapped her arms around a surprised Andre. "Initials C.S."

"Yes? Can you elaborate?" Andre's brows knitted together.

Betsy jumped up and pulled Andre with her. "C. S. is Crab Shak. It has to be it." Betsy broke into a song and waltzed the officer around the table.

"What's all the racket?" Steve appeared with his hair mussed and wearing morning whiskers.

Page entered on Steve's heels. "Why are you both dancing at five in the morning?"

Betsy released Andre and waved a paper in the air. "We solved the secret code."

"Wow! That's fantastic news." Page hurried to her cousin's side. "Show me."

Betsy laid the piece of paper on the table. "Okay. We're working with 0925-2100CS. Andre and I think it translates into September 25, 2100 hours, which is nine p.m. at the Crab Shak."

Steve rubbed his chin, considering the information."

"I see their logic. I believe they've figured it out." Page studied the code. "Yep, I sense you've nailed it. Congrats. Steve?"

"I concur. I lost my cupcake prize." Steve gave Andre a wink.

Page continued with her assessment. "The Shak may

do a mean Po'boy, but it also attracts unseemly types. This we know first-hand from our other cases. It's the perfect place to meet and not look suspicious."

"I owe you an apology, Betsy." Andre's voice sounded contrite.

"An apology? Whatever for?" asked Betsy.

"I invited you to dine at a place with a bad reputation. I didn't know."

"Andre, the Shak serves some of the best seafood at Shell. Besides, I'm the type of gal who likes local color. No apology necessary."

"Wait. I missed something here. You've already scored a date, Betsy Ross? And, in the middle of a hurricane?" Page looked incredulous.

"I'm still a hot chick." Betsy's hands found her hips. "You've got Detective Dreamboat to sail away—"

"Would you please stop calling Tanner..."

Steve motioned to Andre. "This is the place where we excuse ourselves and check our cell phones for messages."

"I think you're right." Andre snagged his phone from the dining table and followed Steve to the porch.

CHAPTER 17

The electricity had kicked on again, shifting everyone to a celebratory mood. A renewed energy to solve Dean's murder trumped the storm's lingering effects. Four bowls of cereal circled the kitchen island, awaiting the claims of weary faces and their spoons. Aunt Tilly's annoying cuckoo clock announced the hour as six. The sounds of chainsaws and trucks from the world outside brought hope that life was finding a normal rhythm. A few gusts continued to rattle the cottage's windows, while the rain had become more of an annoyance than a deterrent.

"I simply must get some stronger tape to keep the cuckoo bird inside his house. I swear I'm about to go cuckoo. He may have won the last round, but I will triumph," declared Betsy, raising one arm in the air. She returned to sprinkle chopped pineapple and pistachios over her cereal.

"My money is on you, Betsy." Steve stirred cream into his coffee and ignored her bowl's concoction.

"My money is on Aunt Tilly paying us a visit if you dare touch her beloved clock again." Page held up a banana. "Andre? Want half?"

"No, thank you. I'm going to head outside and check the road. Those saws sound like they mean business. Maybe I can go before I wear out my welcome." Andre slipped out the door, leaving his bowl of cereal for Betsy to scoff.

"He's a real doll, that one." Betsy took her bowl to the dining room. "Hey, someone bring Barnacle breakfast. Poor guy is sitting in his chair all sad-faced."

Page signaled Steve. "I've got this. Barn, can you eat the leftover stew for breakfast?"

"Ruff."

"He said yes," came the muffled words from Betsy's mouth full of cereal.

Steve's cell phone rang. "Tanner here. Are you kidding? Make sure you thank Officer Handler for me. Tell him to bring the chump in. Oh, and don't bother Koch. He took the overnight shift. I'm on duty."

Betsy twisted around. "Who's the chump? We've met so many in our short time at Shell Isle."

"Antonio Luigi Furazio." Steve hit a button on his phone. "Hang on. Put me through to anyone in IT."

Page sent a shrug in Betsy's direction.

"Mike, Officer Handler is bringing you a challenge. Time is of the essence. He'll provide an explanation, but I doubt you'll need one. Thanks, man." Steve clipped the phone to his belt. "Sorry to eat and run, but I need to see if I can get to the station."

Page snatched his sleeve and tugged him backward. "Hold on there, Tanner. You can't leave until you tell us what's happening."

Steve cracked a grin and kissed Page's cheek.

"Don't go starting up the funny business with me right here." Betsy took her dish to the sink.

"No time for funny business, snoop." Steve released Page's arm. "Okay, here's the latest, and then I need to head out. That dumb-ass Tony refused to hand over the laptop when the guys showed with the confiscation slip. This is the place where you ask, 'What did Tony do?'" Steve paused.

"What did Tony do?" responded Betsy.

"He started jumping up and down on the laptop, trying to destroy any evidence. Fortunately, it has an industrial case. Still, the officer said he managed to inflict damage. He and the computer are on their way into the station. What a chump."

An inkling surprised Page. "Listen, the laptop has everything you need for a motive. It's complicated. Fingers crossed, your IT guys can retrieve something for you."

"Understood, and thanks, Page." Steve opened the front door and assessed the weather. Looks like the worst may have passed. If the officer assigned to you isn't outside, I'll have Andre hang around. I see him across the street talking to utility guys. Later, ladies."

~*~

Page glanced out the kitchen window. "Looking good." She heard Betsy start the dryer. "Hey, hot chick, can you bring out the suspect board? It's past time we get to plotting. I stuck it in the hall closet."

Betsy appeared. "I'm going to ignore the hot chick. You're making fun of me. That slipped out last night. Red lipstick has that effect on my personality."

"Really?" Page quirked a perfectly arched eyebrow.

"Yes, really." Betsy made a face. "About the suspect board. What if Andre comes back and sees our doings?"

"I just watched him and Steve leave. Our babysitter is parked outside in some jalopy, which the rain can only enhance. Let's get to work." Page opened the end table drawer. "Here's the shoebox with supplies. I'll grab the easel from my den."

"Okay, okay. The sooner we get this case solved, the sooner my life takes on new meaning. Hang on. Ina's calling. I need to tell her she's got the day off. Did you let Daisy—?"

"Yep, texted her. Go to Ina. I'll schlep the board myself." Page set things up and even drew pictures of the five suspects. She sat down in Tilly's hideous flamingo chair and vowed to find a replacement before the holidays.

"Sorry. Ina had to expound on having a run-in last evening with two women at the market. She was all hyped up over them cutting in line with their full basket to her single item."

"How rude," said Page.

"Wasn't it? A smirk appeared on Betsy's mouth. "Our Ina threatened to call the store manager. I laughed when she told the feisty one to back off because she was dealing with a Jewish broad. The other woman must have heard wrong. She freaked and asked how Ina knew her friend's name. Turns out the woman's name was Jewel. Get it. J, E, W?"

A flicker of surprise shone on Page's face.

Betsy adjusted her coral bead bracelet. "Anyway, Ina told the two she didn't care what they called themselves because, in her eyes, they were a couple of Shiksas. Ina said you never want to get called a—"

"Get Ina back on the phone," Page ran for her cell

phone.

Betsy looked confused. "Why? I've told you the story. There's nothing more — "

"Yes, there is more to tell. Call Ina while I try to reach Steve."

"But." Betsy pushed the buttons. "I don't — "

"The name Jewel. How many Jewels do you know?" asked an exasperated Page. "She's got to be our suspect."

"Jeez, our suspects' names slipped my mind. We do need the board to get things sorted." Betsy activated her hand fan. "Ina, I'm back. Page needs to talk to you about your encounter with the Shiksas." Betsy tossed the phone to Page.

"Hi, Ina. Listen, I think the two women you had the encounter with are the suspects we've been trying to find. We need to ask you some questions. Hang on a sec." Page turned the speaker on both phones and held them close together. "Steve, are you there?"

"Yeah, I just left you. What mischief have you gotten into now?"

"The best kind. I've got Ina on the other phone. I think she had a run-in with Jewel and Stella last night. Do you want to hear her story and ask questions?"

"I sure do. Ina, can you hear me? Start at the beginning."

Ina recounted what she'd told Betsy, applying a bit more drama to the telling.

"So, you didn't exchange any more pleasantries with the two after leaving the market?" asked Steve.

"Thankfully, no, but you may have some interest in what I observed while sitting in my vehicle. Betsy had to hang up before I told her this part."

"Ina, I'm hanging on your every word," answered Steve.

Page shook her head but stayed silent. Steve was a real charmer with the ladies.

"So, I'm sitting in my car calling my husband to find out if I had time to stop at Ivan's Deli for an egg cream before the weather got worse. Have you ever tasted one of Ivan's chocolate—"

"Ina, get back to the two women," encouraged Steve.

"Yes, so I see them walking toward their vehicle and arguing with each other. Just my luck, they've parked next to me. My window is down so I can hear the exchange. Seems there's someone in the hospital that neither one wants to visit. Can you imagine? Then, they drive away and hopefully to another state. Shell Isle doesn't like loathsome Shiksas."

"Thanks, Ina. You've provided some helpful information. One last question, and it's important. Did you notice what they were driving?" asked Steve.

"Yes, it was blue...and dirty. I always notice dirty vehicles."

"Blue and—"

"Dirty. Listen, Steve, I gotta dash. If I think of anything else, I'll tell Page and Betsy. You keep us safe out there." Ina disconnected.

Page picked up her cell phone. "So, there you have it, detective. Either Jewel or Stella may pay the pretend Dean a visit in a dirty blue car." She couldn't contain her laughter.

Steve groaned. "And I thought being a detective in a

small beach town would ask little from me."

Page's laughter grew louder. "Yep, you're looking for a dirty blue car."

"Listen, you are punchy as hell from a lack of sleep. I'll ring you later."

"Wait!" Page's voice grew louder. "I'm not done. I'll anticipate getting my thank you letter for linking the Ina encounter with Stella and Jewel. Now, how about the ME's report? See if Tony is carrying. I sense the gun may turn up sooner than later."

"All on my list. You do know I've been doing this work for—"

"I've got my own work to do. Later, Tanner." Page beamed at Betsy. "Let's get to that suspect board. This is one time I want to best Detective Steve Tanner."

"One time? You're talking to Betsy Ross, who knows your sleuthing ways. You always sleuth to win." Betsy reached for the colored markers. "I require a recap. This go-around, I pick the colors for each suspect."

Page swiveled her chair to face the easel. "Let's start with Tony since we have some facts to plug in."

"I'm assigning him red because I think he's the one who did Dean. Give me means, motive, and opportunity." Betsy wrote next to the drawing of Tony.

"Tony probably had the opportunity. His alibi with some tart named Velvet hasn't been verified. As for means, a gun to a guy like him is like peanut butter to jelly. What we're missing is a motive. Help me." Page sat back.

"You saw him and Dean arguing at The Perk and the

strange exchange of laptops." Betsy put the cap on the marker.

"Yes, but is that enough to call it a motive? I don't think so. Still, I believe there's a motive that hasn't been uncovered. I'm not a buyer of Tony vacationing at Shell to hang out with his pal Dean. They're not friends. Steve should have more after the IT guys get into the laptop, and he questions Tony again. Let's move on. Who's next?"

"How about Lucky? Not much to write on the board." Betsy grabbed a blue marker.

"I'm going to take the lead with Lucky and say he could very well possess all three. At Movie on the Green, Lucky and Jewel threatened Tony if he didn't shape up fast. They had a concern about his loyalty and abilities. He crossed the line that night and became a liability. There's your motive, Betsy."

"You're right. I'm filling in the motive for Jewel and Lucky. Not Stella, right?"

"Not Stella...yet. Back to Lucky. Do you think he had the means?" Page asked.

"Sure. He's another type like Tony. Guns are a necessity." Betsy recorded means. "As for opportunity, for now, I'd say anyone in the free world could get to Dean easily enough."

"Agreed. Check the opportunity box. To save time, write the exact same for Jewel. More than anyone else, she was down on Dean." Page scrunched her eyebrows together thoughtfully. "The two women's accents are driving me crazy. I can't place them."

"You'll figure out where they're from in time if it matters." Betsy waved the marker. "Jewel gets the evil black marker after messing with our Ina."

Page watched her cousin add the details on Jewel. "Do Stella next."

"I'm assigning her yellow because I always wanted pale blond hair, and you said she had—"

"I never knew you wanted to be blond. How about that? I learned something new," said Page. "Yes, yellow for Stella. Motive? Means? Not showing much there. She's Dean's girlfriend and took up for him."

"Hang on. What girlfriend doesn't want to visit her boyfriend in the hospital?" Betsy tapped the marker in her palm.

"A pertinent question, Bets, and I'll tell you. The type of girlfriend who's worried about becoming a suspect and linked to some illegal activities. So far, Stella gets checked for having the opportunity until she's found and produces an alibi."

"Got it. Last is the philandering Amos Park. I cannot abide cheating husbands. I divorced two of them." Betsy released a heavy sigh. "He's purple cause I'd like to bruise him up."

Page half laughed. "Speaking of you and men, we will continue our discussion about you hanging your bonnet on debonair Andre Lyon. You've got a reprieve because this case is stagnant, and we need to un-stagnate it."

"Thank goodness for stagnation. Andre is so debonair. Isn't he?" Betsy's eyes sparkled.

"It's worse than I feared." Page waved her arms. "Betsy, you cannot get entangled this soon—"

"I'm not entangled. It takes me at least two weeks to fall off the man cliff. I'm older, slower, and wiser now. So, relax yourself. I only met him yesterday. Back to Park the louse."

"Okay, I'll table the Andre talk for now." Page studied the suspect board.

"Do you see Park having the means or motive? I don't. He's a boring math teacher with a penchant for solving complicated formulas and breaking the code to bed women." Betsy left two blanks next to Amos's name.

"I'm still pondering his penchant for formulas. Remember what I noticed on the chalkboard seemed out of place in a classroom." Page waved her index finger.

"That's so easy to explain." Betsy cleared her throat.

Page knew what was coming. "I'm in for another Betsy Ross soliloquy?"

"Yes, you are. I'm reminding you of what I said earlier. Park probably belongs to some geek math club. Follow me here. There are mystery clubs where members take unsolved cases and try to solve them. It's like a hobby. Math or cipher clubs are probably the same." Betsy paused. "Isn't the word *proof* a math term? I'm about to digress. So, I dated this math professor once. He wore the cutest bow ties. What was his name? Herbert? No, it was Hank. Anyway, Hank lived to stump the other professors with hard-to-solve equations. One day we were cuddling and—"

"Stop there. I'll award you it's plausible for the chalkboard equations being some game if you won't say another word about your professor." Page watched Betsy scribble "opportunity." "I think—"

Betsy jumped in. "I betcha Park was catting around that night with the teacher who interrupted your meeting. We know his wife can't truthfully alibi him, but his side honey can."

"I agree she's worth chasing down. Opportunity remains a question." Page smiled in answer.

"Face it. This guy has no reason to want Dean dead. They had nothing in common. Amos Park is a married suburban guy. Dean's a condo guy, new to town, and hanging around some unsavory types. Worst case, they didn't like each other." Betsy sat next to Page.

"Do you have more to add, oh, wise sleuth of Shell?" Page teased.

"Yes, ma'am. I'm becoming top-notch at evaluating suspects. I came over so you could lavish me with compliments and 'atta, girl' pats on the back."

Page lifted an eyebrow. "Is that so?"

"And, to get my fan." Betsy flung it open and lifted the hair from her neck. "Well?"

Page kicked off her navy sneakers. Barnacle quickly snagged one shoe, taking it to his towel. "I forgot he was still here. Have you fed him since he got the dab of stew?"

"It's me, Betsy. Of course, I fed him extra, but I'm leaving the potty walk to you."

Page hopped up to retrieve her shoe and glanced outside. "Barnacle, if I open the screen door, will you do your business and come right back? I don't want to chase you down the beach in this weather."

"Woof." The dog trotted to the door.

"That's Barn speak for 'yes, I will do as you ask. Let me out before I explode.'"

"Really? One woof meant all of that?" asked a skeptical Page.

"Yep. Open the door already. I want to hear your suspect wrap-up speech so I can hide the board. Shake a leg. I need a shower." Betsy stood waiting.

"My wrap-up is one sentence. What I need is an inkling and Steve to score a dirty blue vehicle with occupants. Come on, Barn. You shake a leg, too, or lift it. Your choice." Page released the door and saw Betsy head toward her bedroom. "First time I'm truly alone in hours." The next inkling came. "Well, okay then." She'd been warned.

Page went to the kitchen sink to rinse the cereal bowls and load the dishwasher. She glanced out the window and froze. The officer's jalopy had been replaced by a dirty blue sedan.

CHAPTER 18

Page's mind ran a gazillion scenarios of what to do next. Only one plan made sense. Her police protection had evaporated, and the reason had her addled. Calling Steve wasn't a viable option. By the time he'd show, the blue vehicle would probably be gone just like before. Another strong inkling, followed by a nudge to act, caused her to sway backward. Both seldom came together unless time was conspiring against her.

She heard Betsy sloshing around in the tub, singing her second song in her bath-time repertoire. That meant she had a half-hour. With an impish grin, Page chose her plan of action. Within minutes, an incognito sleuth slipped out of the slider. She walked down to the beach wearing a black raincoat, sunglasses, and hair tucked under a ballcap. The sleuth scurried up the beach access ramp a short block from the cottage.

Page sighed on seeing the vehicle still parked. Approaching it, Page saw a woman's profile behind the steering wheel. Stella or Jewel's interest in her was getting tiresome. With little sleep, Page felt her patience reservoir about empty. Her goal seemed doable. Get the tag number and call Steve.

Writing the last number on paper, Page considered adding to her mission. Maybe she'd march up to the driver's window and say howdy. Yep, she was feeling mighty bold and crazy. "Enough of this intimidation. I'm going for it. I want to know why they're so worried about me." Page kept pep-talking herself toward the car. "There are power and road crews all around me. I'm safe enough. This case needs my help." Out of the corner of her eye, she saw a male presence running toward her.

Page halted by a bucket truck. Two workmen were in discussion over a leaning light pole.

"Is that you under all that garb, Ms. Wright? I'm Officer Webb, assigned to you and Ms. Ross." A young man dressed in jeans and a parka stood a few feet away.

"Yeah, I'm Page Wright. Am I ever glad to know you're out here. I thought something had happened to our protection when I noticed your jalopy gone."

"Jalopy?" Officer Webb frowned.

"You know, the vehicle you're driving incognito?"

"Sorry. I'm in that black pickup parked over there," Webb pointed out.

"Then, who was driving the rattletrap which spent the night parked outside my cottage?"

"I wouldn't know, ma'am, as I replaced Detective Tanner a few minutes ago, and it wasn't there."

"Weird. Listen, since you're here, let's go visit the blue sedan. Steve and Koch have been looking for it. Trust me, you don't want to miss this opportunity." Page took a step and felt a hand on her arm.

"With all due respect, Ms. Wright, I can't let you approach the vehicle. Please return to your cottage, and I will make contact once I see you're safely away." Officer Webb's tone had changed to all business.

"But I'm a sleuth and consultant on this case, and I can help —"

"With respect, I need —"

"Okay, you've shown me enough respect. I will agree to wait here. You might need my assistance. That's called compromise."

"I'm not sure." Webb glanced at the sedan and grabbed his phone.

Another inkling came. "Make that call. Now! License number South Carolina, JAM 686." Page chuckled to herself, thinking a jam was what the occupant was about to find herself. She heard Webb request backup.

Within seconds, the car's engine started. Page's instincts kicked in. She reacted by running down the sidewalk toward the driver's side. Out of breath and her face wet from the rain, she tapped on the window. She could hear Officer Webb approaching.

The dark glass slid down into its track, revealing Jewel's surprised face. "You?"

"Yep, and wondering why you're so interested in little ole me? I don't know what you're about, but you picked the wrong woman to mess with. Go harass someone else, or better yet, leave Shell Isle. Furthermore, whatever you did the other night at the marina has you plenty worried and me plenty curious. And, trust me, you don't want me to be curious." Page's eyes shot unlethal daggers.

"Excuse me. Ma'am, I need you to shut off your engine

and step outside," instructed Webb.

Jewel glared at the officer, then stomped the gas pedal. The sedan's tires spun wet sand over Page and Webb.

Page spat out sand and wiped her face as she watched the car speed away. "This would have gone a lot better if you hadn't butted in."

"With all due respect, you could have gotten shot if I hadn't butted in." Webb secured his gun in the holster. A glob of sand sat on his cheek.

"With all due respect, you'd better let Detective Tanner know the dirty blue vehicle is on the move...again. You're about to experience his wrath." Page tightened her raincoat and stomped toward Hibiscus and a hot shower.

"Good grief, Page, you look like a drowned rat that played in a sandbox. Don't tell me you had to chase Barnacle down the beach?" Betsy stood at the front door wearing her fuzzy purple bathrobe.

"Barnacle? Oh no. I forgot about him." Page pivoted and took off, running toward the beach, hollering his name. "Steve's going to act more than chapped if I've lost his dog," huffed Page, coming onto the beach. She looked in both directions and was rewarded by seeing a lonely police car driving in the distance. "Where in ding blazes are you, Barn?" Page turned toward Steve's bungalow.

Lifting the gate latch in his backyard, Page entered. "Barnacle, are you? Why, yes, you are!" Page peered into the doghouse's door. A familiar furry spaniel face stared back. "I'm so sorry I left you outside. You can't tell Steve." Page patted his head. "You were smart to come here and get out of the weather."

"Ruff." Barnacle ventured out and licked Page's hand.

"Come on home with me. I'll cook you a giant serving of ground beef and toss in a new chewstick as a bonus.".

"Ruff, ruff."

"Ah, I think you said yes twice. Let's go, boy."

Page made her second entrance inside the cottage with Barnacle on her heels.

Betsy had changed into a fall-colored broomstick skirt with an orange jersey top. "So, are you planning another fast exit, or might you stay and face the music coming your way?"

Page hung her raincoat and cap on the metal hook in the foyer. "I'm staying put. I need a hot shower and a cup of calming tea." Page passed by Betsy. "Hang on. What music coming?"

"Steve rang your cell phone, and when you didn't answer, he called mine. He gave me an earful about you confronting a suspect outside. Expect a dressing-down visit from him any moment."

"I hate those dressing-down talks about police business versus our business." Page grabbed a napkin and dried her face.

"I tried to calm him down. I told him even you wouldn't do something so dumb, but he wasn't having it."

"Oh, I'm dumb all right, but his officer acted dumber. I was this close to getting somewhere with Jewel." Page held two fingers an inch apart. "And, that rookie officer came—"

That's Detective Dreamboat leaning on the doorbell. Go shower. I'll get the door and serve him my version of a calming brew."

"While you're pouring tea, throw some ground beef in the microwave for Barn." Page took off toward the shower. "I was so close to plucking the honey badger Jewel's last nerve," she mumbled to herself.

~*~

Page entered the kitchen and saw Steve parked on the barstool while Betsy washed Barnacle's bowl. Both males look too contented. "What gives?"

Steve gazed at Page with a loopy expression. "What gives, you ask? Something Betsy doused my tea with has me all—"

"Mellow. He's mellow, probably for the first time since he sucked in a breath. Enjoy it while it lasts." Betsy poured more brew into Steve's cup. "There's a good boy. Drink up."

Page peered closer at him. Laughter threatened to escape as she watched Steve fail to prop his cheek on his hand. His head hit the island with a thud. "I hope he isn't needed at the station. He's pretty much useless right now. Betsy, this time you may have gone too far."

"Too far. Ya think?" Steve parroted. "Think."

"About him being needed? His cell phone has rung a few times. He couldn't seem to punch in the right buttons, so I shut it off. We took care of that little prob. Didn't we, detective?"

Steve mustered another loopy look at Page. "I can't focus right. You have six aqua eyes. They're pretty, but there are so many of them." He pointed a finger toward Page and counted out loud. "One, three, seven...."

Betsy spewed soda out of her mouth.

"What's wrong with his vision?" Page glared at Betsy.

"He'll be fine soon. Maybe I should take the tea from him?"

"There's a good idea." Page grabbed the mug and sniffed. "Dare I ask what's in your potion?"

"It's my special recipe of herbs." Betsy dipped her index finger in the cup and tasted the tea. "I made it for this sexy linebacker I was once dating. He had trouble with too much testosterone, not that I thought so. This one night we were—"

"I beg you, no details. How soon will Steve behave normally?"

"Probably not in this lifetime, cousin. He's got Seal in his DNA."

"Betsy? I'm not joking. How long? I'm taking him to the station because I bet Tony's still waiting for the grilling."

"Thirty minutes tops. Stop fretting." Betsy draped the white dish towel over the sink faucet.

"Did she say I'll recover in dirty minutes?" asked a confused Steve.

Page touched his arm. "Thirty minutes. You'll feel yourself in thirty minutes."

"That's what I thought she said. Thirty minutes? Wanna hanky panky while we wait?"

Page bit her lower lip. "Betsy Ross, I swear on Tilly's cuckoo—"

"This is when I disappear to my bedroom and answer emails. The sun keeps trying to say hello, so maybe we can open Honey Bees in a bit?" Betsy made her escape.

"Come on, handsome; let's get you to work where Koch's black coffee will restore you to acting like the—"

"The detective who arrived to give you a talking to for the dumb stunt you pulled. You should never approach a suspect's vehicle. One, four, no six aqua orbs."

Page watched as his lucid moment faded.

"I hope dirty minutes hurries up. Take me to Koch's coffee pot." Steve accepted Page's arm to guide him outside. "I'm arresting Betsy for…something."

"Of course, you are. I'll help you figure out what later." Page tucked him into her SUV's passenger seat and fixed his sunglasses. Behind the wheel, she glanced around. The jalopy was back.

CHAPTER 19

By the time Page delivered Steve to an amused Koch, the tea's effects were waning and replaced by plots to pay back Betsy. She wanted to discuss the jalopy with the detectives, but needed Steve to have all neurons firing.

Page managed to steal a glance inside the vehicle as she drove past, but the driver held up a newspaper, blocking his or her face. By process of elimination, she knew it wasn't Jewel or Tony. That left Lucky or Stella. Amos Park wasn't a fit for anything but philandering and possessing an attitude. And, if Betsy and Andre were right in breaking the code, Dean had a rendezvous at the Crab Shak tonight. A meeting he wouldn't make. Would someone else fill in? She heard her name but missed what Koch said.

"Sorry. I was somewhere else. Could you repeat what you said?" asked Page.

"Daydreaming, snoop? Never mind, I asked if you wanted to sit in on our little chat fest with Tony? Don't feel obligated to—"

"Page never misses a chance to gather clues." Steve squinted at Page. "You only have four eyes now. Things are improving."

Koch chuckled.

"Steve's right, except for the *snoop* remark. He means

sleuth. Yes, I need more clues. A lot more. Should I head to the observation room?" asked Page.

Koch turned to Steve. "Are you in good enough shape to do this?"

"Yeah, but I need more coffee. The damn tea has me so whacky. You may need to arrest me later for killing Betsy Ross. Get the wise guy in here." Steve poured another cup and downed it.

Page patted Steve's shoulder as she passed. "Make me proud, Tanner."

Moments later, Page settled into the observation room chair. Hearing her cell phone ding, she glanced at the text from Betsy announcing she was baking cookies at Honey Bees. With any luck, she'd join her cousin within the hour. With Ina not there to supervise Betsy in the kitchen, Page fretted what spicy cookies might find their way to the bakery display.

Movement in the two-way glass caught Page's attention. She watched Tony get escorted into the interrogation room. He wore the surly expression well. Steve and Koch assumed their usual stance. From appearances, Steve seemed back in control. Betsy was correct. The tea's effects lasted a half-hour, but not Steve's wrath.

Steve activated the recorder and Mirandized Tony for the second time. "Okay, Tony, you've got some explaining to do." Steve straddled a chair. "Let's start with the jumping on the laptop stunt. Not your best move."

Tony lifted his double chin. "I told you the laptop has private business stored. I was simply protecting my employer's confidential dealings. I don't know why you're harassing me. I told you I had nothing to do with Dean taking a bullet."

"Yes, you've been vocal on that point. Our IT team has the laptop in the lab." Steve looked at Koch. "Any updates on how they're coming with extraction?"

"Yes, sir. I understand they're close to breaking the encryption code."

"Excellent." Steve stared at Tony. "Why not save us all time? Tell me what information pertains to Dean? Of course, if Dean is awake, you and I can still pay him a visit, bring the laptop along, and see if he wants to identify you as the one who shot him. Yep, we can play it that way, too."

"I told you. No hospitals. I've got PSDT." Tony grabbed a napkin from the table and wiped his forehead.

"How about two easy questions? What exactly is your job? Who's your employer?" asked Steve.

The door opened, and Koch accepted a paper from one of the IT engineers. He scanned it quickly before passing it to Steve. "Good stuff here." He sent a smirk to Tony.

"Well, this information is nicely timed." Steve handed Koch the note. "So, I can help you with some answers, Tony. You work for Dean's father as what I'd label as his bulldog. Plus, an FBI buddy of mine had a chat with Mr. Arthur Minnto earlier today. He was forthcoming in supplying information."

Surprise combined with worry colored Tony's features. He said nothing.

"You see, Tony, I already have answers to some of my questions. I'm giving you the chance to come clean and fess up to what you're doing in our town."

"I explained I'm vacationing and hanging out with my pal, Dean."

"But that's a lie. See? You're not taking advantage of my good nature and offer." Steve's fists clenched, signaling Tony that he'd run out of rope.

Page watched as Tony considered his next move.

"Listen up, you chump, I'll give you one last chance. You can take this personally. You don't fit here, and we don't want your type here. The sooner you can make a case for your innocence, the sooner we'll give serious thought to providing you a nice escort out of Shell Isle. Of course, charging you with breaking and entering, along with document counterfeiting, remain strong options. Koch is a fan of option two. Do it right here, and maybe you can go to Miami and handle whatever shady real estate dealings you're doing for Mr. Minnto. What's it going to be?"

"Give me a minute here. I gotta collect my thoughts." Tony's eyes darted to the exit.

"Don't even think about adiosing, amigo," threatened Koch. "There's more of me right outside this door."

Page got a welcomed inkling. She signaled the officer outside her door to call Steve.

"I'm desperate and tired of playing peek-a-boo with this thug," Steve said, appearing in the doorway. "Give me something, and I'll consider sparing Betsy's life."

Page gave a short laugh. "Ask him why Dean and his father have different last names."

"I figured Mintto was a stepfather. No?"

"Nope," said Page.

Giving Page a salute, Steve hurried back into the interrogation room. "Alrighty, Tony, while you're considering my other questions, I've got another one. Why does Dean's father have a different last name than Dean? Don't give me the stepfather lie."

Tony shifted in his chair and looked at the floor. "Could be Dean Westin isn't kosher as they say."

"As in Dean's using a fake identity?"

"Maybe." Tony's Adam's apple moved up and down like a yo-yo.

"He gotcha, wise guy," mumbled Page.

"I think I understand the so-called friendship you have with Dean. Those fake IDs you were trying to retrieve are part of a side gig you work. You provided Dean with a new identity, which allowed him to become Dean Westin, a math teacher licensed in South Carolina. I wonder if Minnto knows you helped his son? How am I doing so far?" Steve scribbled a note to Koch and waited for him to leave.

"I didn't say I gave him the ID. He could have stolen them along with the other ones." Tony's expression shifted to confidence. "Maybe he procured them elsewhere."

"Nah, you would have pitched that scenario first. I'm not a buyer. For whatever reason, Dean, or whatever his real name is, needed to become someone else. You've got the answer."

"If I do, you're not getting it."

"Know what else I discovered? Dean's father's business is commercial real estate in Chapel, New Jersey."

"So what? Nothing illegal in owning real estate, last

time I checked." Tony's attitude returned.

Page shook her head. "Not a good strategy, Tony. You're messing with a cunning fox."

"You're right, buddy, but it's illegal to hike rents monthly and shake down tenants. I'm a betting man, and I bet you're a big help in this department for Minnto."

"Pure speculation, detective." Tony looked bored.

"It's speculation only for the moment. "My FBI friend told me they discovered Minnto has been doing this for years. They plan to dig deeper. It's not good to have the Bureau's attention. Yes, sir, their spotlight is on him, thanks to you and Dean's little vacation meet-up. Minnto won't like you messing things up."

Page saw the confident expression drain from Tony's face.

Steve delivered another strike. "Hey, don't feel left out. I've got the Shell Isle spotlight aimed right at you. Your list of illegal activities is becoming impressive." Steve glanced at Koch.

"I'll say. I'm keeping a list of charges right here." Koch pointed to his temple. "Breaking and entering, selling fake IDs, shooting his pal over some misunderstanding. There's one more —"

Tony jumped up. "I did not shoot Dean. Listen, I can't discuss Mr. Mintto's business dealings with yous. I'd be a dead man walking out of here. You know how these guys operate. I'll own the fake IDs and welcoming myself into Dean's condo, but nothing else. I doubt with your limited resources in this beach dive, you want to fool with those petty charges."

"Sit down, Furazio." Koch got in Tony's face. "As I was saying, I have one more potential concern on my list to check out. We discovered in the pat-down that you've got an empty ankle holster. Since we got the ballistics from an independent crime laboratory on Dean's bullet, we're enthusiastic about finding your gun. Where is it, wise guy?"

Tony shrugged in indifference. "I lost it."

Koch turned to Steve. "The officers didn't find anything in his motel room or the rental he's driving. Dean's furnished condo is clean except for the laptops and some classified ads and scribbled numbers."

Steve nodded. "He's hidden the weapon somewhere. We'll find it and probably match it to the bullet."

"You wish. So, are you going to charge me with those nothings or let me go?" Tony smoothed his pants.

Steve ignored Tony and addressed Koch. "Charge him. Be sure you find him the right roommate."

"Are you frickin' kidding me?" Tony shook off Koch's attempt to escort him out.

"Those words just sealed your fate. You're about to make friends with Salvatore. He's a bouncer from the next 'beach dive' town. I'll warn you, he's got quite a temper." Koch opened the door.

"I want my own cell! I have rights!" Tony's voice boomed in the hallway.

"Yes, princess. Come along to meet your handmaiden." Koch winked at the officers he passed.

Steve motioned to Page. "Wanna lift to Honey Bees?"

"Thanks, I'll take you up on the offer." Page grabbed her handbag.

An officer approached Steve, excitement dancing all around him. "Detective Tanner, we flushed out a suspect. Operation Flush worked."

CHAPTER 20

Steve halted. "Fantastic. This case is turning our way. Where did you nab—"

"At the hospital. A guy attempted to doctor our pretend Dean with a syringe full of who knows what. I was outside the door, acting the orderly role. Good thing I was, because it took both of us to cuff him."

"Excellent work, officer. Where's your 'doctor' now?" asked Steve.

Page started to do a U-turn back into the observation room, but Steve's hand on her elbow stopped her.

"Getting booked around the corner. If it's okay, I'd like to change outta this hospital garb and back into my uniform?" the officer pointed to the orderly's white pants, which were three inches too short. "The guys here are sure to razz me."

"See to it. Thanks for some fine police work."

"So, when do I get to find out who you snagged, Tanner?" Page poked him in the ribs.

"Stand here for five seconds, and I'll bring your answer back with me," replied Steve.

"Better hustle. I'm counting. One thousand, two one thousand...." Page knew Steve's timer was flawed when he hadn't returned after a full ten minutes. She walked outside to wait and check in with Betsy.

"Betsy, I should get to the shop soon. How are things going?"

"We're busy. I guess with so many without electricity, they're coming here for pumpkin sustenance. Hang on a sec," said Betsy. "Those cupcakes have to go in a box and not a bag."

"Um, Bets, just who are you instructing in cupcake care?"

"Oh, Andre is here helping me. It's his day off. He stopped by to make sure Webb was on duty and watching out for me. Anyway, Andre saw how busy I was, and the sweet man offered to pitch in. Listen, I gotta go." The oven timer went off. "I baked my latest and greatest cookie recipe. Wait, the cupcakes need —" Betsy clicked off.

Page rolled her eyes. She didn't know which troubled her most. Andre being smitten with Betsy or some insanely spicy cookies offered to customers. Where was Steve? She needed to get to Honey Bees, even if it meant hitchhiking. A strong inkling came. It felt like a warning.

Within seconds, the blue sedan pulled up next to Page. "Get in." Jewel's tone carried a warning.

"I'm not getting in your car." Page's mind clamored for what to do.

"Maybe this will encourage you." Jewel pointed a pistol at Page. "I'm a good shot. Don't act stupid."

Page climbed in the backseat and barely got the door closed before Jewel sped around the back of the police building and parked.

Page returned to an upright position. "What do you

want with me? I'm getting tired of — "

Jewel twisted to face Page. "Shut up and listen." Her steely voice matched her eyes. "Your amateur snooping is targeted at the wrong people. I'm giving you one last chance to cease meddling in our affairs. Return to your bake shop, and you'll live to sail with your detective another day. If you don't do as I say, you'll miss the next sunset. Now, get out before I change my mind."

Page said nothing and clamored to open the car door. Once she was out, Jewel sped away, leaving Page dumbfounded but alive. She walked quickly to the front of the police building.

"Where have you been? Touring the parking lot?" Steve waited by his vehicle.

"Yeah, I felt slighted that I've never been given a proper tour of the facility grounds. Jewel was kind enough to drive me around back and provide her version of a tour." With trembling hands, Page reached for the handle. "And for the record, I hate dirty, blue sedans and occupants waving guns at me."

Steve came around and wrapped his arms around Page. "Are you kidding me? Jewel nabbed you right here at the station?"

Page nodded and sniffed.

Steve knelt down by the open door and reached for Page's hand. "I'm thankful you're okay. If something ever happened to you, Sherlocka — why the hell did you leave the safety of the station without me by your side?"

She felt the first tear slip down her cheek. "Because it

smells like stale coffee and disinfectant in there. It gives me migraines. Betsy offered to smudge the place when we were working on Captain Jake's murder, but—" Page gulped. A big cry was coming, along with the reality of what had just happened.

Steve held her close and punched a button on the phone with his free hand. "Find the damn blue sedan. It was just in our parking lot. On our turf, the suspect, Jewel, threatened Page. I haven't gotten the details yet. She's pretty shaken." Steve tossed the phone in the driver's seat and offered Page his handkerchief.

"Thanks." Page dabbed her eyes. "The kindly Jewel has given me one final warning to stop meddling in their affairs, or I'll miss the evening sunset. And, you know how much I love Shell Isle sunsets."

Steve touched her cheek. "I promise you many more evening sunsets are in your future, but you must make me a promise." He tilted Page's chin. "Look at me, please."

"What kind of promise?" she asked, feeling a sob rising in her throat.

Steve tucked a strand of hair behind Page's ear. The gesture calmed her spirit. "Promise me you won't go off again without an officer or me by your side. Can you please make that promise?"

Page crossed her fingers. She felt an emotional boost wash over her. A nudge followed. "Okay." Buoyed, she leaned back into the seat, reminding herself that the inklings protected her. They always had, and for a moment, she'd forgotten the fact. Her gifts served to right the wrongs of others. Cowering away defeated the service she was meant to give.

"Page?" Steve stroked her arm.

Feeling renewed, she looked at Steve, "I'm back, and I reject the dose of fear Jewel delivered. Yep, I'm feeling mad as a wet hen and ready to talk." Page told Steve the details of the encounter.

"At least Jewel kept it brief and didn't take you off somewhere. You had a close call, Page Wright, and you don't want any more of those." Steve closed her door.

She waited for him to get behind the wheel. "Hang on a sec." Page covered the ignition button with her hand. "Before you spirit me off to Honey Bees, who tried to inject pretend Dean? You haven't said."

"It was Lucky. Who, incidentally, isn't feeling so lucky this minute, but someone else is."

"Lucky." Page mumbled to herself. She needed the suspect board and some quiet to noodle this latest information. Did Lucky act on his own? Did he act on someone's direction? If so, who? "Hmm, Lucky."

"Hello, Page?" Steve waved his hand in front of her face. "That look tells me your sleuthing genes are activated."

"Don't worry. I'm only digesting the info. Hang on. Who is it feeling lucky?" asked Page, removing her hand so Steve could start the engine.

"Tony, full of baloney, has made bail."

Page laughed. "Tony, full of baloney. Good one, Tanner. He made bail?"

"Yes, and the fastest we've ever had one of Koch's room

reservations get canceled." Steve smiled through narrow eyes.

"But who—?" Page pulled out her sunglasses.

"Another goon type appeared. Clearly, some powerful strings were pulled to get Tony out, which adds to my concerns around this case. I was delayed leaving because I approved the press release of Dean's death. We've snared our man."

"Maybe. Maybe not, detective," replied Page.

"Hey, Sherlocka, it's looking good from my side. Lucky was carrying a 9-millimeter handgun, which fires the same size bullet our ME pulled from Dean." Steve turned the SUV toward Main Street.

"I grant you, things don't look good for Lucky." Page popped a piece of gum in her mouth.

"Stress relief?" asked Steve.

"Yep, but it involves Betsy's unsupervised cookie baking, which I'm about to confront."

"Excuse me. I need to check something." Steve gave a voice command to dial Koch. "Is Webb still on protection detail?"

"Nope," answered Koch. "Andre knows we're short-staffed because of the storm, so he's parked at the snoops' bake shop. He forfeited his day off. I like our new guy."

"I heard you call us snoops, Koch. No more free donuts for you." Page said, teasing.

"A mere slip of the tongue, lass." Koch laid on a brogue.

"Enough, you two. Let me know when Lucky gets on the hot seat. Unlike Knuckles—correction, Tony—no one can check Lucky out with a charge of attempted murder. Also, let's make sure the word gets out. We're buying info on a Crab Shak meeting tonight."

"Later." Steve pulled up in front of Honey Bees. He put on his flashers.

"Thanks for the lift. I'm really okay. Jewel rattled me, but I'm protected by my inklings and Shell Isle's finest. I remain resolute to find Dean's killer and get back to enjoying running our shop and—"

"Sailing with me?"

Page leaned over and kissed Steve's lips. "Most definitely sailing with you."

"You can call me Detective Dreamboat if you like." Steve returned the kiss.

"Let me out of here. I've got to deal with the big blabbermouth who thinks a spicy cookie is a delicacy."

"Stay safe and don't venture out of the shop until closing. Say okay, Detective Tanner."

"Okay, bossy Detective Tanner." Page stepped out.

"Hey, play your cards right, and I may update you after I interview Un-Lucky."

"Tanner, I'm expecting you'll ask for more of my invaluable help. You'd better play your cards right. Ta, ta." Page waved and went in search of the pumpkin aficionado.

A busy Betsy was helping two young girls choose brownies. "You should try these lip-smacking pumpkin ones with cream cheese frosting." Betsy pointed to the display case.

One girl wrinkled her nose. "I'd like the chocolate, please."

Page caught Betsy's eye and waited for her to finish.

"Here you go, two chocolate brownies and one pumpkin for you two to share. It's my treat. Let your taste buds experience a new adventure." Betsy handed the bag to the girls. "Enjoy."

"Finally, you show. I've been covered with customers." Betsy took a sip of her iced tea. "We may have to close early because the cupboard is almost bare."

"We'll figure something out. Maybe Ina left some treasures in the second freezer." Page walked toward the kitchen. "Follow me back, and I'll share my little dose of excitement with you and Andre."

"Excitement? That's why you're late? I don't like your brand of excitement. I'm not sure I want to hear about it." Betsy trotted behind Page.

"Hi, Andre." Page froze. Dumbfounded, she watched the officer vigorously whisking a mixture in a stainless bowl. "What's going on? Betsy, explain."

"Hi, Page. I can explain. I'm making Betsy's new recipe for ginger spice tarts. I told her of my affection for them. It's a French favorite, you know." Andre went back to mixing.

"Ah, yes." Page nodded and yanked Betsy into the hall. "You do realize you have a police officer who's technically on duty performing as your pastry chef? And, what's that in poor Andre's hair?"

"First, it's only some flour. I didn't have the heart to tell him when I opened the flour bag that a cloud of it landed in his hair." Betsy let out a giggle.

"Honestly, Betsy Ross, some days I—"

"Hold up. Let me finish. Second, Andre's capable of

reacting to any problem that befalls us, whether he's got a whisk in his hand or a gun. I find him most nimble."

"Nimble? I surrender this day to the Honey Bee gods." Page threw her hands in the air and went in search of Ina's frozen stash of baked goods.

"What about your excitement story?" hollered Betsy.

"Later."

~*~

Page took stock of the display case, now brimming with Ina's thawed jam-print cookies and macadamia chip mini-cakes. The apple walnut strudels looked so delicious that Page had snuck one for herself. A wise Betsy and Andre had remained in the kitchen, whipping up what Page couldn't begin or want to imagine. The bell rang, signaling customers entering.

Surprise found Page's face as she watched Amos Park and Principal Holly heading her way.

CHAPTER 21

"Well, well, we meet again. Sorry, I don't remember your name." Principal Holly stood on the other side of the counter.

"It's Page Wright. Welcome to Honey Bees. How may I help?" She noticed Amos was distracted by his cell phone and hadn't approached.

"Amos and I had a late lunch meeting at The Bistro. I wanted to stop in and buy a dozen cookies for when I watch tonight's televised soccer match. My sweet tooth has called me all day. Let's see, what to choose?" Holly peered inside the case.

"I brought out the oatmeal cranberry cookies a few minutes ago. I've sampled them and can attest they're yummy." Page watched the teacher from the corner of her eye. He seemed agitated as his fingers tapped the phone's screen. A page from a newspaper he had folded under his arm fell to the floor. She watched Park ball it up and toss it in her trash can. Page received a nudge. This time, she was clear about what action to take. "Would you like a sample?"

"Thanks, but no sample to awaken the beast. I'll take the oatmeal cookies. Amos? Oatmeal or chocolate chip?" Principal Holly glanced toward the teacher when he didn't get a reply.

"Get me two dozen of the espresso chunk." Park continued to tap his phone.

He's lost in the screen," offered Page. "We're out of espresso chocolate chunk. Why don't you let me mix the bag with a dozen oatmeal and chocolate chip for him?"

Holly nodded. "Sure, that'll work." He placed the money on the counter.

Park never acknowledged Page but waited at the entrance for the principal. Maybe he didn't remember her. She watched both men exit Honey Bees. Page hurried to snag the newspaper from the trash can. She was smoothing it on a display table when the dynamic baking duo appeared from the back. Page shoved the paper in her pocket. No point in setting herself up for another lecture from Betsy. She'd gotten the extended version after recounting the Jewel meeting. Page plastered a relaxed smile on her face.

"You simply must taste this tart." Betsy passed the plate to Page. "I've positively outdone myself. Right, Andre?"

"I must admit they are quite good, though way too much work if you ask me." Andre untied his apron and hung it behind the cash register on a hook.

Page took a tiny bite. She'd been burned by Betsy's culinary debacles too many times. She stared at the tart with a discerning eye. "Gracious me, but this apple tart is pure heaven. You made this?"

"Well..." Betsy cut her eyes toward Andre.

"We both had a hand, so to say, in the tarts." Andre winked at Betsy.

"Yes, I think I can detect what part your hand played,

Andre." Page's eyes danced. The man could bake a mean tart. At least the flour was gone from his hair. She heard her cell phone ringing in the distance.

"I've got to eat one more," declared Betsy.

"You do that while I answer my phone." Page pulled it from her handbag. "Hello, Steve. We were about to close for the day. What's up?" Page put him on speaker so Betsy and Andre could hear.

"Would you like to do a double date at the Crab Shak tonight?" asked Steve.

Page's face lit. "Double date as in Betsy and Andre and you and me? And we're going there because tonight is when this secret meeting is to take place between Dead Dean and some unknown?"

"Yes, and yes. I was able to squeeze out of a tight lip Lucky that the Crab Shak is indeed the place named in the classified. I've also obtained solid information from Lucky, his cell phone, and further inquiries. This case finally has serious forward movement. I'll bring you up to date with what I can later. You game for a double with extra plain clothes officers around us?"

"On two conditions. One, you're buying, and two, I don't have to play pool. Those bikers aren't my type." Page bobbed her head when Betsy gave a thumbs-up. "Oh, Betsy and Andre are in."

"I will accept your conditions, Sherlocka. Let's all meet at Hibiscus around eight for a powwow. Andre will see you both home safely, and Webb's pulling a double shift. He's got snoop—uh, sleuth—duty until I show up. I'm reminding you not to venture out of Hibiscus. Are we good here?"

"We're good, Detective Tanner. You bring the goods on Lucky tonight. Our suspect board has never looked so pitiful. Ciao."

Betsy emptied the cash register. "It's quitting time. Looks like we've got to plan for a Crab Shak outing."

Andre held the display case door while Betsy put the remaining cookies in a sack to take home. "And I thought I'd take you to the Crab Shak for a tasty seafood dinner. Instead, it's turning into a reconnoiter mission. Not exactly what I had in mind when I invited you out, Baker Betsy."

"Baker Betsy, is it?" teased Page. "I like it. Sounds like you need to wear a white smock. We'll have to see about getting it embroidered with 'Baker Betsy'."

Betsy elbowed Andre. "Now, see what you've done? She's paying me back for calling Steve—"

"Betsy…Aunt Tilly always said, think before you speak," threatened Page.

"I think I won't speak. I'll eat cookies instead. Let's go home. Lead us out, Andre." Betsy munched the first cookie.

Andre escorted the women toward the door and flicked off the lights. "I need a shower after my afternoon at baking school." Once outside, Andre nodded to Webb. "See you, ladies, at eight o'clock sharp." Andre Lyon sent a smile to Betsy and headed to his vehicle.

Page acknowledged Webb. A flicker of irritation shone in her eyes.

Betsy sashayed past the young officer and bestowed a wink.

"Honestly, Betsy. I already regret releasing you from the no-men moratorium."

"Hush. It's all harmless fun," Betsy pointed out. "I parked across the street."

"Yep, I couldn't miss your bright yellow hatchback on a moonless night."

"Can I help it if vivid colors speak to my soul? You, on the other hand, drive a boring white, vintage British—"

"Eat another cookie." Page stowed her tote in the backseat and caught a glimpse of Amos Park strolling along the bayside walk toward the same red-headed teacher who'd appeared in his classroom when she visited the school. If the woman's skirt was any shorter, she'd need to find a certain street corner.

"Isn't she the strumpet you suspect Amos of having a dalliance with?" asked Betsy.

"The very same. I need to ask Steve if he checked out Amos's lying alibi. Get us home. We need to refresh the suspect board. I'm texting Steve questions now. Surely, he can give us some morsels before tonight's double date. We'll need a big block of time to process the information, so don't start whining, Bets."

"No whining, but may I ask an itty-bitty favor of my dearest, sweetest, most—"

"What is it?" Page half-smiled.

"Could we spend a measly hour in our loungers on the beach? The sun is out. The storm is a memory, and we have the time to spare since we closed at four today."

"Absolutely. I love your idea. We must cram in as

much beach time as possible before it turns cold."

~*~

"You bring your novel with Dowager Margaret, and I'll tote our chairs." Page opened the storage closet outside her porch.

"I've got the book and two bottles of juice." Betsy came along the side, wearing a big smile under her sun bonnet.

"Just swell," groaned Page as she took the steps down to the beach.

"What'd I miss now?" Betsy glanced around.

"Webb. I forgot about him." Page tilted her head in his direction.

"Geez, the poor sap is traipsing in the sand wearing dress boots and socks." A laugh escaped Betsy.

"And he's supposed to be undercover." Page rolled her eyes at him. "I see a training opportunity."

"An opportunity for Steve, not you. Page, you're not going over to Webb?"

"Take the chairs. I'll join you in a minute." Page marched toward the officer. The closer she got, the less steam she had left. He was young and learning the ropes. She'd thrown him a curve by not staying in the cottage as Steve had asked. She hung a left and caught up with Betsy.

"You handled the training pretty pronto. Help me unfold—"

"We've got to go back to Hibiscus," said Page.

"What? I haven't read the first page to see if the dowager found a new cook."

"Listen, Betsy. I forgot Steve asked us to remain inside

until Dean's murderer was caught and Jewel is dealt with, too."

Betsy took off toward Hibiscus at a fast clip. "Webb, make haste!" hollered Betsy. "Get thee over here. I need escorting, and so does Page!"

"So much for undercover," said a breathless Page, catching up. "The last time I saw you move this fast was when a kid tried to show you his pet frog."

Webb came alongside. "Ladies, I'd appreciate it if you wouldn't pull a stunt—"

"Momentary lapse. Comes with age. It won't happen again." Page shoved the chairs back in the storage closet and headed for the screen porch.

"Yeah, we messed up. I'm going to make it up to you. I bet you're hungry, and you've come to the right cottage. You park yourself wherever you're supposed to, and I'll bring you an early dinner plate," proclaimed Betsy.

"Thank you, Ms. Ross. I haven't eaten since breakfast." Webb headed for the picnic table.

A grin tugged on Page's lips. The karmic wheel was about to visit Officer Webb. She followed Betsy inside.

~*~

Page pulled the board out of its hiding place. "Betsy? Aren't you finished dressing yet? The whole point of us getting ready early was so we'd have time to—"

"I'm here. How do I look?" Betsy did a pirouette.

Page did a double-take. Betsy had pulled her unruly mop into a French twist and secured it with a daisy clip. Lip gloss and a matching coral shade of blush brought a feminine glow to her perpetually flushed face. The uncharacteristic choice of flowing black pants and a cream top created a casual, put-together look. Her cousin had dressed for a date. "You look lovely, Betsy."

"Thank you. It seems we both chose black britches. I'm sure Andre will appreciate my French twist, emphasis on *French*. He's growing on me, despite being a copper."

"He seems like a grounded type of guy and very polite. Andre is definitely a departure from your past colorful entourage."

Betsy poured peanuts into a bowl. "You threatened me with men picker school if I didn't—"

"Let's focus." Page turned to the suspect board. "Bring your nuts and grab a seat. We've got to figure out who-dun-it to Dean. Steve answered my text questions, so we've got new info to plug in."

"Tanner must really feel desperate to invoke our help." Betsy shoved a handful of nuts into her mouth. "Start by telling me about Dean."

Page nodded. "Here's what we know about him. Dean was the new math teacher. He arrived at Shell using a fake ID, which somehow managed to evade the school's HR background check."

"Must have been a first-rate match-up for Dean to fool HR. The bad guys are getting really good at this stuff nowadays." Betsy's mouth turned cynical. "What else about Dean?"

"Steve said their interviews with his peers proved Dean didn't mix with the teachers. No one had formed much of an opinion of the guy. It was as if Dean wanted to appear invisible. The *ghost teacher* title Principal Holly bestowed on him fits."

More nuts went into Betsy's mouth. She squinted at the board. "That's because Dean was involved in shady dealings with Jewel, Lucky, and Stella. He didn't want any attention. And those shady doings were tied to the classified ads. They signaled him for his meetings, where he passed some kind of code to his contact. Right?"

"You got it. Get a load of this scoop from Steve. I'm going to read what he sent." Page reached for her cell. "'Lucky's phone was a real find. He, Stella, and Jewel are involved in corporate espionage. We traced calls to a pharmaceutical company headquartered on an island off Greece. I can't pronounce the company's name, so we're calling them Zeus.'"

"Wow. Good stuff. Zeus. Wasn't he the big boss of the other gods?" asked Betsy.

Page gave a brief laugh. "Don't digress, but yes. Remember how I couldn't place Jewel and Stella's accents?"

"Greek, right?"

"Bingo. Here's what I'm intuiting. Someone working at the nearby LRN Laboratories is feeding pharmaceutical research secrets to our bunch. Somehow, Jewel and the team hooked up with Dean and his expertise to decode the information before sending it to Zeus. We know Dean got antsy and wanted out. That gives Lucky, Stella, and the ring leader, Jewel, plenty of motive. Agreed?"

"For sure. They're swimming in treacherous water with pharma sharks. Jewel saw Dean as a liability she couldn't afford to keep. The company she was spying for could just as easily eliminate her if they sensed their operation compromised. For Jewel, it was about self-preservation." Betsy's tone grew more confident. "I'm getting too good at this sleuthing."

Page nodded and kept adding info bullets next to Jewel and Lucky.

Betsy clapped her hands. "Plus, you know first-hand Jewel's got a gun."

"Up close and personal, I got to see that gun and not just any gun. A nine-millimeter handgun. Jewel and Lucky both carry weapons matching the bullet size pulled from Dean," added Page. "At least Steve has Lucky's gun to check, but not Jewel or Tony's…yet."

Betsy went to the fridge and grabbed a soda. "So, Lucky and Jewel have the motive to keep working for Zeus and stay alive."

Page wrote on the board. "Yes, they have a strong motive.

I see Lucky as Jewel's do-boy. He's the one who'd do the deed, and that's why he showed up at the hospital to kill Dean again." Betsy paused. "I had no idea drug espionage was so—"

"Lethal," supplied Page. "Yes, think about how expensive medicines and treatments have become over the years. New formulas that get approved make these companies more powerful and rich. Power breeds greed. Principles get sacrificed for the bottom line."

Betsy turned as the cuckoo appeared, announcing half-past seven. "I hate that bird."

Page smiled in answer. "Pay attention. We're going to star Lucky and Jewel with motive, means, and opportunity, and move them to the top of the list. Jewel is in position one because it was likely her directive to Lucky—"

"To adios Dean," finished Betsy. "Let's consider Tony. He's my floater."

"Floater?" Page held the red marker designated for Tony and turned to her cousin. "This is a new sleuth word. I can't wait for you to elaborate."

"A floater is a suspect who can float up and down on our suspect board depending on the facts we gather. In the case of Tony, alias Knuckles, he remains my primary suspect. Please continue." Betsy waved her hand.

Page nodded. "Here's what Steve said, 'Velvet, the lady of the night Tony claimed to have been with, checked out to a point. Being drunk, Velvet could not validate the time she left Tony's room. Koch is reviewing the motel security camera footage.' So, I'm sensing Tony probably had the opportunity. As for means, his gun is missing, but we know he owns one. It's hidden for a reason."

"Right. That leaves motive." Betsy set the peanut bowl to the side.

"Tony's got a tepid motive that I sense is about to explode into a powerful motive to take out Dean. We need to wait for more clues and information. I agree with you; Tony's flirting with our Numero Uno slot. For now, he's sitting in position three." Page placed the marker in the box.

"I choose Stella next. She's a yellow pen," supplied Betsy.

Page nodded. "Stella was Dean's squeeze. Like you, I rank her low for the murder. It's not like Dean was the type to fool around and get her jealous. No, I see Stella's role as a minder of Dean."

"Ah, a minder. It fits. Dean would let his guard down with Stella, and she could gauge his loyalty and skills and report back. Our Jewel sure runs a tighty ship."

"I believe it's a tight ship, Bets."

"Whatever. You need both tight and tighty ships. Stella lacks a killing motive."

"Agreed." Page left the box unchecked. "What about means and opportunity?"

Betsy gave a huff. "This is one of your tricks to see if I've learned the sleuthing rules. You always say a motive drives the means and opportunity. So, if Stella lacks motive, why would she kill Dean?"

"Indeed, she would not. Gold star to Betsy Ross."

Betsy stood and did a curtsy. "Move on to Amos Park and the purple marker.

Page uncapped the purple marker for Amos. "We'll start with motive. What's his?"

Betsy's expression looked blank. "He's not very attractive, and yet he lassoed a wife who likes spas. And he's got a side hussy. I can't think of a single reason why this math teacher would give two ticks about Dean. They had nothing in common except for teaching ciphering."

"True," said Page.

"Did Steve give you any info on this guy?"

"Yep. He confirmed what we knew. Koch scored a hit

with Amos's wife when he threatened to charge her if she provided a false alibi. She sang louder than a canary about Amos staying out for the second time in a week." Page smiled in satisfaction.

"He's so busted." Betsy gave a scoffing laugh. "It's up to his strumpet to alibi him."

"She was a touch fuzzy on the exact time she and Amos were cuddling, but insisted they were barking up the wrong tree," added Page.

"Sure, Amos has a quasi-alibi for opportunity, but the means is unknown. None of that matters because Amos lacks—"

"A strong motive to kill Dean." Page checked "means" and "opportunity" with a question marks to the side.

"Well, so much for him and his loose zipper. Still, we'll keep him on the board because I don't like cheaters." Betsy peeked at her watch. "We'd better hurry."

~*~

Betsy went to the foyer mirror and tucked a stray curl. "We always have one or two suspects who act as our red herrings. I think Stella and Amos qualify in this case."

"They appear to."

"Was that a vehicle door?" asked Betsy.

"Quick, hide the board. No way are we showing Tanner our sleuthing methods." Page waited for Betsy to open the closet door. An inkling came calling.

CHAPTER 22

"Evening, ladies. Are we ready for the night's festivities?" Steve entered Hibiscus and offered Page a hug. "I had to sneak off from Barnacle otherwise he'd—"

"Uhm, said pooch is already in the porch hammock," Betsy pointed out.

"You've got to be kidding me. This isn't your second home." Steve motioned for the dog to come.

Page had to laugh. "Oh, but it is. Remember, he has an assigned place at the table. You can't say that, Tanner."

Steve opened the front door just as Andre went to knock. "Come on in. I've got a wayward dog to take home."

"Not a good night for you, Barnacle," said Andre, stepping inside. "Hello, Shell Isle sleuths. Ready to gather clues?"

Betsy stood aside for Andre to pass. "I suppose. The sooner we get this case solved, the sooner I can get back on my beach lounger. In fact, tomorrow is my day off and—"

"You're off tomorrow?" asked Page.

"You forgot I traded with Ina so she could host the ladies' bridge club." Betsy looped her arm through Andre's. "You haven't met Ina Funk yet. Didn't I tell you she's my assistant baker, good friend, and bowling buddy?"

Andre nodded. "Yes, you did. I look forward to

meeting this Ina…Funk. Though her name—"

"Is hilarious," finished Betsy. "We love our Ina, don't we, Page?"

"Most certainly. Ina is a huge asset to Honey Bees, as is Daisy Koch." Page invited Andre to take a seat.

"Would Daisy be any relation to Detective Koch?" asked Andre, choosing the flamingo swivel chair.

"Yes, Daisy is Koch's daughter." Betsy lighted on the white wicker chair closest to Andre.

"I'm back," declared Steve. "Webb is taking off, but he asked if you had any antacids. I saw him taking an empty paper plate to the trash can."

"He must have really enjoyed the meal I made him. How nice," said Betsy.

"Um, what did you feed him, Betsy? I need my men able for work," Steve said through gritted teeth.

Betsy's cheeks flushed. "I call it Kicker Stew because the spice—oh dear, I must have overdone the poblanos a smidge. It just registered; he needs antacids."

Steve peeped out the door. "He's bent over in the flower bushes. Hurry and get the chews."

Page handed Steve four tablets. "Trust me."

The three sat and said nothing as they waited for the detective's return.

"He'll live to eat another day." Steve returned, shutting the screen door.

"That's a relief. Mental note, Betsy. Fewer poblanos next time." Betsy tapped her temple.

Steve grabbed a soda from the fridge. "Let's get back

on track. I promised a further update on Dean's case before we head to the Crab Shak."

"Come join us." Page patted the sofa cushion next to her.

Steve's eyes glanced around the room. "Don't you want to bring out the suspect board?" He turned to Andre. "These two ladies manage to secret away their sleuthing tools. One day, I hope to catch a glimpse of this infamous board. It must have some kind of Ouija juju."

"Sounds intriguing." Andre laughed as he spoke. "I'll keep my eyes peeled for a sighting, detective."

"Okay, enough of the wisecracks. Give us the skinny. I'm starving and craving a shrimp po' boy." Betsy stole a peek at Andre and reached for her fan.

"We're making real progress now. I'm hopeful we can close the file in the next forty-eight hours. Here's the latest to add to what I texted earlier." Steve woke his phone and glanced at his notes. "Koch returned to Principal Holly for another chat. This time, Holly was willing to share Amos Park gossip."

"Oh, I do love me some juicy gossip," said Betsy. Her hand fan speed increased.

"It seems Amos has been showing interest in the computer science teacher."

"Another dalliance. He's a busy one. That's a tasty morsel," exclaimed Betsy.

Page grabbed the nearby notebook and pen. Judging by his good mood, she sensed Steve had plenty to share.

Andre's brows drew together. "How's this guy

attracting women? He's not exactly winning for best-looking teacher."

"Simple. He's chumming the tarts with my delicious cookies," answered Betsy.

"Ignore her," Page said, pressing a hand to her forehead. She refused to acknowledge the migraine pain. "Attraction is a complicated emotion. Continue, Steve."

"I'm saving Lucky's update for last since we're pretty confident he's the one who shot Dean and came back for an encore. Tony's been busy. We've had him under constant surveillance. The wise guy who made Tony's bail has stuck to him like glue. They checked Tony out of the motel in a hurry."

"Where did they go?" asked Page.

"That's the rub. We don't know. They managed to give us the slip while tailing them. It should never have happened. The officer said that when Tony came out of the motel room, he had been roughed up pretty badly and was limping to the vehicle."

"Poor Knuckles and all for a laptop," said Betsy.

"What did you say, Bets?" Page sat forward.

"I said poor Knuckles and all for a—"

"Yes, laptop." Page felt the excitement build with her intuition. "The laptop is the key to what's gone awry for Tony."

Steve looked confused. "I'm going to need you to elaborate a bit more."

"It's becoming clear to me. Dean had a laptop that Tony came to Shell Isle to confiscate. Tony works for Dean's father, who has shady real estate dealings in Jersey. Yes.

Give me a sec to place some more puzzle pieces." Page grew quiet, waiting for more insights to come. She knew the earlier inkling had yet to reward her, but having the gift of filling in blanks with her intuitions would hasten solving this twisty murder plot.

No one spoke. Three pairs of eyes were held captive by Page.

Page tapped the pen on the notebook. "And Dean was likely involved with the family business. We know Dean wants to run when he gets nervous."

"I can verify Dean worked for his father for the last few years. My FBI buddy supplied me with this fact. He also said Dean was shaking down some of the weaker store owners for cash before he disappeared," said Steve.

"I think I see where you're going." Andre nodded. "You're suggesting Mintto sent Tony to find his son—"

"And more importantly, the laptop, which I'm betting had private files on Mintto's dealings. That's why Tony was attempting to stomp the computer into oblivion. I've no doubt really incriminating information that gets someone prison time is stored in it." Page took a breath. "Remember, I witnessed the unpleasant laptop exchange at The Perk? Tony came for the computer."

"Regretfully, I failed at getting you to ignore the exchange. Now, here I sit in the middle of another murder case, and you having been threatened at gunpoint by some maul named Jewel." Betsy's voice held a tremor.

Page patted Betsy's arm. "I'm fine. This will end soon."

Andre reached for Betsy's free hand and held it.

Page, you're saying Dean's downfall came from his possession of laptops. His plan must have been to use the laptop files as protection from his father's wrath. Disappearing to Shell Isle and teaching high school math gave Dean what he thought was anonymity," Steve said in a deliberate voice.

"I'm stuck at figuring out why Tony and Dean would exchange laptops. It should have been a one-way exchange. Dean passed Tony the laptop with Mintto's illegal doings. Yet, I saw a second laptop move across the table. Curious." Page felt her mouth tense.

"Lookout, you two. Something's coming," informed Betsy.

Page felt a flush. "Listen, Dean possessed two laptops with information worthy of being murdered. The question is, who got to him first the other night?"

"The correct answer lies with the ballistics testing of the guns. Unfortunately, we're a small police force and had to send the bullets to an independent lab for examination," answered Steve.

"Yes, usually the weapon points us to the murderer. Will it deliver this time? It's too soon to say." Page's tone sounded wistful.

Steve stole a glance at his watch. "We've got enough time for me to finish the Lucky update. Maybe having this additional information will seal Lucky's fate for you, Sherlocka."

"I'm all for sealing ol' Lucky's fate by tonight. My beach day tomorrow would be perfect." Betsy squeezed Andre's hand. "I'm already feeling the sun."

"Spill it all, Tanner. I've got a doozy of a migraine trying to invade my evening, and I need dinner." Page massaged her temples.

"Let me finish the Tony tale by saying they tore out in a silver rented SUV with a broken left taillight. We've got a police car at the bridge, the only exit off Shell Isle. The mayor wouldn't approve a vehicle check, so this is the best we could achieve. If they want to go adventurous and leave by boat, we've got a couple of guys at the marina watching."

"Where I hail from, that's what we call a tight close," said Andre.

"We're fortunate in this situation that Shell Isle isn't easy to leave unnoticed. We placed cameras on the causeway years ago to monitor things since it's a drawbridge."

"Makes sense to me," answered Betsy. "Could you talk faster? Page has a migraine, and I have a big hunger about to erupt."

Steve smiled in answer. "Anything for you, duenna. The best news is we found Tony's gun hidden in the motel's HVAC duct. I suspect the wise guy was calling the shots, and Tony decided to avoid more trouble. He left the gun behind. It's in the police lab with Lucky's. We'll have the report tomorrow afternoon, and I think a murderer booked."

"Time for Lucky talk now?" Page went to the kitchen and poured a glass of tea. She popped two aspirin and returned to the sofa. "My pen's ready to write. Give me something."

"When you hear all of this, you'll see why we're convinced Lucky is our man." Steve inhaled. "Late this afternoon, Lucky's public defender copped a plea deal.

Lucky admits to working for Zeus to steal secrets from LRN Laboratories. They've got a lab rat planted there who's been supplying the drug trial formulas. The rat is the one placing classified ads when he's ready to hand off the next batch. Lucky says the tech copies the code onto a laptop and passes it to Dean. Once Dean unravels the cipher, Jewel encrypts everything to Zeus."

Page received an insight. "It's making sense to me now. I know what happened. Dean messed up and somehow gave Tony the Zeus laptop. That explains the heated exchange at The Perk. Tony thought he'd been duped by Dean." Page stared off. "Of course, that's the explanation. Dean was a real dufus and mixed up the machines, which doesn't add up. Pardon the pun."

"What's that mean?" asked Andre.

"Maybe we don't want to know," said Betsy.

"I don't have that answer." Page sighed.

"Let me wrap this up so we can leave. Lucky admitted that the three of them are in our country illegally and with fake IDs. He refused to tell us how to find Jewel and Stella."

"Big surprise." A sardonic smile beamed in Betsy's eyes.

"Hang on. Lucky did tell us tonight's meeting is to deliver the final formula. After Jewel gets it, she and Stella are catching a flight, but Lucky wouldn't say from what airport or what they're driving. He has no idea who Jewel will send in Dean's place. Lucky said she and Stella were behind a closed door, working out details, when we caught him at the hospital. Here's the last piece. Lucky maintains he didn't kill

Dean the first time but was sent to finish someone's botched job. More he wouldn't say."

"Detective Tanner, I congratulate you on some fine work and in such a short time. You've got loose ends to tie up. Lucky is smart enough not to confess to murder, but an attempted murder charge could have him out of prison before his hair turns completely grey." Andre shook Steve's hand.

"Thanks, Andre. Legal is checking on what laws apply in Lucky's home country. We still need to find Jewel and Stella. As it stands, we have three individuals planning to leave Shell within hours. Time is pressing in on us."

Page bit her lip. "Can't they rush the ballistics report?"

"Koch tried and hit a snag. The stereo microscope needs a new part. The private lab has to wait before they can proceed. So, there you have it, folks." Steve rose and extended his hand to Page.

"I still think it's Tony," said Betsy, moving off with Andre toward the door.

"Maybe the Crab Shak will provide our next piece of evidence. Get me and my migraine in front of an oyster po'boy." Page flicked on the foyer table lamp and closed the door. Another inkling followed her to Steve's SUV. Someone out there had better start worrying.

CHAPTER 23

The Crab Shak boasted the tastiest crispy fried seafood at Shell Isle and competitive pool games happening in the side room. Hubcaps and biker memorabilia decorated the walls, while peanut shells added crunch to the floor. The booths were constructed of reclaimed varnished wood with rock-hard seats, which encouraged a brisk turnover of diners and more jingle for the Shak. Pewter tankards had pounded knicks into the oak tables by enthusiastic patrons. Country music provided the backdrop for an occasional two-step by a few of its regulars. Unfortunately, the restaurant had become a magnet for Shell's shady types to meet.

"Wow, this place is rough and tumble." Andre's eyes glanced around the dining room.

Betsy's face crinkled in amusement. "You ain't seen nothin' yet. Here comes our favorite waitress."

"Now, Betsy. Behave," said Page, bestowing an elbow in Steve's ribs.

"You both need to behave—hiya, Velma. There's four of us tonight." Steve tucked his arm around Page's waist.

Velma, with her bleached blond hair, moved in closer to Steve. Her chest arrived before she did. "What's your pleasure tonight, sexy detective?"

"See? What did I tell you?" Betsy whispered to Andre.

"How about that corner booth over there?" Steve pointed out.

"You got it, handsome. Follow me, everyone." Velma grabbed four menus and swayed her hips toward the booth. "Here you go. Tonight's special is the Clam Po'boy with onion rings and slaw. I'll grab ya some waters while you peruse."

Andre watched Velma disappear through the kitchen door. "That's a lot of woman stuffed into that uniform."

"Just be thankful her roving eye hasn't landed on you," said Betsy. "She lives to flirt with Steve, despite me giving her a talking to about Dream—Detective Tanner having a thing for Page."

Page felt her face color. "Betsy, hush and open your menu."

Steve leaned over and kissed Page's cheek. "I don't have a problem with Betsy saying—"

Page bopped him on the head with the menu. "Enough, both of you. Andre, what looks good to you?"

"Um, I'm going with the fried cod basket. I'm a cold fish guy."

Betsy turned her gaze on Andre. "I sure hate to hear you're a cold fish. I thought—"

"I'm back to take your order." Velma placed the glasses of water in front of everyone. She grabbed her pad and pen and lifted an overarched eyebrow.

"Just in the nick of time. I'd like the Oyster Po'boy with curly fries, but no slaw. Oh, and lemonade." Page handed her menu to the waitress.

"I'll have the same," said Steve.

"And for my big eater?" Velma zeroed in on Betsy.

"I hate it when you call me—never mind. I want the Shrimp Po'boy, an order of large fries, and a chocolate malt." Betsy looked expectantly at Andre.

"Hello, Mr. Dapper. You're quite an entrée yourself. I'm Velma."

Andre cleared his throat. "I'm having the cod basket, and a malt sounds good to me."

"I'll see to your order personally." Velma's cleavage leaned down low enough to touch her toes to take Andre's menu.

Page's eyes followed the waitress to her next victim, seated a few booths away. "We managed to order without a scene. That bodes well for our dining experience."

"To think I invited you here for dinner as a first date." Andre shook his head.

"Where else could you get a sideshow for free? It's all quite merry," answered Betsy.

"Says the big eater," teased Steve. "Listen up. It's time to engage in our mission. I did a visual check of the dining room while everyone was ordering. I don't see anyone acting suspicious. Even the bikers seem subdued in the pool area. You three look around."

"I got nothing," answered Betsy.

"How about those two men at the table by the jukebox?" asked Andre.

Three pairs of eyes turned.

"They're local salty dogs. Nothing to them but some lingering fish smell," replied Steve. "Page?"

"Not yet. What time is it?" A chill washed over Page.

Steve glanced at his diver's watch. "Almost nine o'clock."

"All I ask is that the shenanigans wait until I have my dinner." Betsy reached for the bottle of ketchup.

Andre looked questioning.

"I'm anticipating." Betsy grabbed extra napkins and fashioned a bib.

"I'd say so," Andre said, placing the pepper shaker by Betsy.

"He's one fast learner," Page whispered to Steve.

He reached under the table and clasped Page's hand. "What about Detective Dreamboat? Is he a fast learner?" Steve whispered back.

A sudden sigh escaped Page's lips. "His timing is lousy."

"Such defines the bloke's night," lamented Steve.

Page felt a nudge. "Perhaps not." She released his hand. "Steve, I need your key. I left my cell phone in your vehicle."

"Excuse us, folks. Page is under the delusion she's going outside without protection." Steve rose and extended his hand. "Madame, shall we?"

"Fine, but I didn't need your—"

"Yes, you do." Once away from the booth, Steve's hand stopped Page. "Inkling or nudge?"

Page bit her lip. "How did you—nudge. Let's go." She stood in the sandy parking lot, trying to sense something… anything. Her eyes caught sight of the unexpected. Page pointed. "Bingo on those nudges. Check it out, Tanner."

"What am I looking at?" His eyes narrowed.

"The jalopy parked to the right under the oak tree."

"Is that the same jalopy you keep seeing outside Hibiscus?"

"The very same. Let's go take a peek." Page took a step and felt herself pulled back.

"Let's play this my way. I'll go take a peek, and you go back inside and tell Andre," instructed Steve.

"But it was my nudge that got us here." Her freckles danced on her cheeks.

"Page." Steve's tone grew stern.

With a toss of her honey-colored bob, Page marched toward the restaurant's entrance. Before going inside, she glanced back. Steve had crouched behind a row of cars. She needed Andre outside fast as a backup.

The hostess approached Page as she entered. "How many in your party?"

"My party is already here. Thanks." Page made a beeline for the booth. "Betsy, where's Andre?"

"Gents' room, why?" answered Betsy. "Where are you going? You just got here. Where's Steve?"

"Tell Andre we're outside investigating the jalopy," said Page over her shoulder. She broke into a trot. She couldn't leave Steve without support. Feeling the defense spray in her pocket, Page scoped out the parking lot. The stillness was foreboding. "Where are you?" she whispered. Page moved toward her last sighting of Steve. A strong hand gripped her forearm and pulled her down. "Let go, you —"

"Quiet, Sherlocka. What the hell are you doing back here? I told you to get Andre." Steve's voice held anger.

"He was indisposed. So lucky you have me, after all. What did I miss?" Page tried to peek over the bed of a pickup truck they were hiding behind.

"Stay put. Someone's in the jalopy talking on a cell phone," said Steve.

"What did you hear?"

"I don't speak whatever language—hang on. The car door is opening. Damn, the thing squeaks. It's a jalopy."

Page covered her mouth as the giggle escaped.

"Hush. Okay, raise up a little and tell me if you recognize the person."

Page snuck a glance and slid down the side of the truck. She nodded and smiled. "It's Stella on the move. Come on. She's going in the side door to the pool room."

"You go back inside and tell Andre. I'll go around back and make sure things are quiet back there. The Shak has too many exterior doors. Understand our plan?"

"Yep. Be careful. I sort of like that mug of yours." Page brushed her lips against his and took off. She waved to the hostess in passing. Spying Betsy alone at the table, Page released a heavy sigh. "Is Andre still in the Gents?"

Betsy made a big show of looking around the booth and under the table. "I guess so. Maybe the poor man suffers from intestinal issues."

"What have you fed him today?" asked an exasperated Page. "You about killed Webb with the Kicker Stew." Seeing Stella take a seat in the pool area, Page didn't wait for Betsy's reply.

"You're leaving again? Here comes Velma with our baskets. Am I to eat my Po'boy alone?"

"Looks that way to me, feisty pants." Velma set the food on the table and tucked the empty tray under her arm. "What else do you need? Another bottle of ketchup? Another date?"

"Stowe it, Velma. Go chase after the tattoos in the pool room." Betsy squirted a generous serving of the red sauce onto her fries and watched her cousin.

Page casually ambled over and chose a seat next to a biker. The location allowed her to observe Stella.

"Hi there, little lady. Lookin' for some action?" The silver chains attached to his belt rattled as he faced Page.

"No action for me. I just want to watch." Page swallowed when she caught sight of a knife hanging from his belt. The man took belt use to a new level.

"What's your name? Mine is Cueball." He rubbed his shaved head and grinned.

Page noted the missing teeth and swallowed again. "I'm Page." *Where were Steve and Andre? What should she do? Sit here and pretend to be Cueball's conquest?* At least Stella was married to her cell phone screen and didn't seem inclined to leave.

"Page. I kind of take to *P* names, but I see you more as Peanut." Cueball studied Page's face. "Yeah. Baby, you're definitely *Peanut*. Hey, guys, come over and say hello to our *Peanut*."

Shock washed over Page as four burly bikers headed

her way, bringing leers on their faces. She saw Stella look up, mildly amused as the men circled in front of her.

Cueball pointed to the first biker with long black hair and a matching feather tucked in a headband. "This here is Hawk."

"Nice feather," blurted Page. *What in all that's holy made her say that?*

"You want to hold it?" Hawk reached up.

"No, no. It needs to stay right where it is for admiring." Page's eyes darted back to the dining room. Betsy waved, grinning.

Cueball spoke. "Say hello to Gunner, Tank, and Back Door. These are my riders."

Page managed a nod. Drat, the guys were blocking her view of Stella. "Very nice to meet you all."

"Okay, you've met Peanut. She's off-limits. Go play pool." Cueball turned his focus on Peanut.

Page glanced toward Stella's location and froze. She was gone. She saw Velma making the rounds and heading into the pool room. Maybe her rescue was imminent.

"Honey, what ya doin' in here with my boys? You've got your own man looking for you." Velma wrapped her arm around Cueball's head and kissed it.

Cueball pinched Velma's fanny, never taking his eyes off Page. "Could be Peanut is bored with her ol' Man. What about it? Wanna cut out with me?"

Page drew a shaky breath and found her gumption. She was over her head with this bunch, and the waitress knew it. "Thanks for the invite, but Velma's right. I'd better behave.

Catch ya later." Page hightailed it back to Betsy.

She heard Velma and Cueball sharing a laugh.

"Did you score one of those loud-mouth bikers for me? Or do you want them all for yourself, Peanut?" teased Betsy.

"Pay attention and stop eating for five seconds. Why hasn't Andre returned? Have you seen Steve? Stella just left, and they need to stop her." A breathless Page felt her migraine reach a new level of pain.

"Relax. There must be another illegal poker game happening in the back. Our coppers are likely busting it up. I'm about to eat your cold sandwich."

Page felt another nudge. "Forget my sandwich. Steve and Andre are in trouble. We've got to find them."

CHAPTER 24

Page and Betsy stood outside the men's restroom door. "Heads or tails." Page flipped the coin she kept in her pocket.

"Tails. I always pick tails," sighed Betsy.

"It's heads. I win. You go into the Gents, and I'll head out the back and look for Steve. Ready?"

"No. Why can't we knock on the poker room door first? I don't want to go into the Gents and see and smell... things." Betsy wrinkled her nose and backed away from the planked door.

"Betsy, get in there. I got a nudge. There's trouble, so be careful."

"How I hate those nudges and inklings. They've ruined more meals—" Betsy opened the door. "Woman in the house!" she hollered.

Page hurried outside. She noticed the parking lot floodlight was burned out. "Strange." The moon hadn't yet made an appearance, so she waited for her eyes to grow accustomed to the darkness. Page crept down the ramp to the gravel lot. Hearing a groan, she pulled the small handgun from her purse and moved toward the sound. "Is that you, Steve?"

"Yeah, over here by the dumpster." Steve was face down and trying to sit up.

"Oh my gosh! What happened? Let me help you." Page steadied him as he rolled into a cross-legged position.

Steve rubbed the back of his head. "Damn, this hurts. Someone came up from behind and conked me."

"Let me take a look." Page touched the swelling. It's a goose egg. We need to get ice on it and maybe an X-ray."

Steve stood hanging onto the dumpster for support. "Ice, yes, X-ray, no. Are you and Betsy okay? Where the hell is Andre?" He winced, taking a step. "Stella?"

"Betsy and I are fine, but Stella gave me the slip. I just sent Betsy into the men's restroom to find—"

"Let's get back inside. We're vulnerable out here." Steve grabbed Page's hand and pulled her behind him. Opening the door, he collided with a wild-eyed Betsy.

"I found Andre. I need you to talk some sense into him."

"What's his problem?" asked Steve, reaching for the restroom door.

"All I can figure out is he's trapped in the stall. I can't get the door open, and talking seems like a problem. Hurry." Betsy and Page followed Steve into the men's room.

Betsy pointed and whispered, "That one."

"Andre, It's Steve. What's going on in there, buddy? Need some help?"

"Mmmm. Mmmm."

"Could be a yes," said Betsy.

Steve yanked the wedge from the handle and pushed against the solid planked pine door. It pushed back.

"Hang on, Andre." Steve turned to Page. I need a

couple of muscular guys to help me bust this door down. Can you go out there and find me —"

Page nodded and disappeared.

Cueball and four bikers barreled their way into the restroom. "Peanut said you needed some muscle. I brought plenty. What's up?"

Steve looked momentarily confused. "Peanut? He called you Peanut?"

"She'll explain later," said Betsy. "Guys, bust down that stall door! One of Shell Isle's finest is stuck in there."

"Yes, ma'am," said Cueball. He and the bikers took turns throwing their shoulders into the door. The wood splintered on the third try.

No one spoke for a few seconds at the scene, staring back.

Andre sat with a bungee cord wrapped around him, securing him to the throne. A dirty cleaning rag was draped over his head.

A grinning Cueball pulled the towel away and assessed the situation while the bikers roared with laughter.

Duct tape covered Andre's mouth and eyes. Wiggling on the toilet seat, he managed another, "Mmm."

"Hold up. We'll have you out of here in a minute." Steve pulled his pocket knife and bent over to try to cut the cord. A wave of pain moved through his head.

Page grabbed Steve as he slid down the wall. "Steady on, ol' man. You're getting an X-ray." She wet some towels and pressed them to his forehead. "Don't try to give orders. Cueball's got this."

"Cueball? Peanut?" Steve's eyes glazed over.

"He's got a concussion, and that's if he's lucky," said Page, watching the men free Andre.

"Pull the tape off his mouth fast," instructed Betsy. "Careful with the eyes. Better let Andre remove that tape."

Cueball stepped back. "You're a free man. Stand up. Like your Old Lady said, you can take the tape off your own eyes. Our work here is done. Back to the poolroom."

"Old lady," huffed Betsy.

Page shook her head at Betsy.

"Thanks, whoever you all are. The rest of your beer tonight is on me." Andre let Betsy lead him to the lavatory.

"We'll take you up on the offer. Peanut, join us once you get him situated."

Page smiled and nodded. "Cueball, hang on a sec. I need to ask a quick question. Did you notice the blonde sitting in the corner?"

"Yeah, a real cold wench. She shunned Gunner. Told 'em she was meeting someone and to get lost. Why do you ask?"

"Did you happen to see who she was waiting on?"

"Actually, Gunner did when he went out to check his bike. Someone motioned to her from the parking lot. Right, Gunner?"

The biker nodded. "Couldn't see no face, though. It was a male."

"As for me, I saw her shoot out of the pool room like I sent the eight ball to the side pocket." Cueball made a sound to mimic a pool ball moving.

"Okay, thanks again, guys." Page made eye contact with each biker.

"Sure thing, little Peanut. You're welcome in the room anytime." Cueball's fingers tipped Page's chin and left.

"Peanut? How do you know these guys? Damn my head." Steve failed at his first attempt to stand.

Page ignored his questions. "Come on. Give me your keys. You're getting a picture made. Betsy, can you and Andre find a way home?"

"No problem. Micky and his buddies are here eating. He'll give us a lift back to Hibiscus." Betsy inched the last bit of tape from Andre's eyes.

"Hello, world. It's good to be back. Thanks, Bets." Andre went to Steve's side. "Go get checked out."

"Wait. First, tell me what happened. We're losing valuable time."

"I was in the stall and ready to leave when I heard two men enter. They were talking about Zeus, and then they got quiet. I realized the stall door design had side gaps that would allow them to see me. I immediately hopped up on the tank so I could listen. I knew it must be the exchange going down."

"What happened next?" asked Steve.

"I heard a snap on a bag, and then one guy said, "Lab rat, I'm here to get the last code." I heard someone counting money out loud. So, I know they made the deal. Next, I had a little mishap. They never spoke again."

"That's when you got made?" Steve's voice was tinged with pain.

"Yeah, and the part I'd like to skip over with ladies

present. It involves a faulty zipper."

"I'll worm it out of him later," threatened Betsy.

"No way." Andre shook his head at Betsy. "I heard one of them grab something from the broom closet in the corner. I expect it was the tape and bungee in there. I hadn't latched the stall door, so they came in and threw that towel over my head. Again, no other words were spoken from the time they found me until they left. Andre looked at Betsy. "Didn't you wonder where I was?"

"I thought you had intestinal issues. My husbands all suffered—"

"Not now, Betsy," said Page. "Andre, we're so sorry we didn't act sooner. Steve and I were both outside watching Stella."

Steve leaned against the paneled wall. "So, these two guys made the last handoff, and we blew another opportunity. Clearly, they found a replacement for Dean. Did you get a good look at them?"

"It was quick but good enough to pick them out of a lineup."

"Get an officer assigned to Hibiscus for the rest of the night. Call Koch and tell him you're coming in with a report. And...what am I missing? I can't think straight."

"The interview part," said Andre. "Don't worry. I'm going to interview the patrons and workers before I leave. Maybe someone saw the two guys, Stella, or something helpful." Andre pulled more glue from his mouth.

"Good plan," said Steve. "With any luck, I'll see you at the station in an hour or less."

Page tapped Steve's forearm. "Excuse me. You're coming home with me so I can keep tabs on you, assuming they release you from the hospital clinic. No sleeping with a concussion. Let's go, detective. Move slowly. I don't want to see you splat on the floor."

Betsy looped her arm around Andre's. "You're with me. I'll introduce you to Mickey. Prepare yourself. Our ride home is a dune buggy."

Andre's brows grew together. "Can this night get any better?"

"Or perhaps Peanut could arrange you a ride with Cueball," offered an amused Betsy.

"Or perhaps I can arrange a personal trip for you on Back Door's bike, blabbermouth Betsy. Unlike Cueball, he's got most of his teeth for chewing your culinary creations." Page volleyed, sensing the night was not done with her.

CHAPTER 25

"Give me your key?" Page put her hand out.

"With the pain killer in me, I feel fine. It's only a mild concussion." Steve met her gaze.

Page wiggled her fingers. "Gimme, Tanner."

"Fine." He dropped the key into Page's palm and went to the passenger side.

"So, here's the plan." Page backed out of the hospital parking place. "You're coming to Hibiscus for the night."

"I don't—"

"You can't complain about sleeping on Aunt Tilly's settee because you're not allowed to sleep until five a.m., sayeth the doctor. You and I will eat some supper and wile away the wee hours trying to figure out how to find Jewel and Stella. You've already got traps set for Tony."

Steve made another attempt. "I don't—"

"I'm not done. You will do the ice compresses and not complain." Page flicked the turn signal on and felt a strong nudge. She gripped the steering wheel tighter.

"I hate ice. I don't—"

Page broke off and took a deep breath. "What else is there to say, Tanner?"

"I say fate has turned our way. There's Stella's jalopy up ahead. Step on it." Steve grabbed his phone and called for backup.

"You're not up for this encounter," said Page, drawing closer to the vehicle. "I'll follow them until the officer catches up."

"No, you're going to play this my way, Sherlocka. I'm tired of being bested by these suspects. The women are on the run to catch a flight. Remember?" Steve switched on the vehicle's hidden blue flashing lights. "Let's see if they act smart and pull over."

Page didn't know what Steve had in mind, but she trusted his instincts even under the influence of painkillers. He was Seal tough.

"Smart lady. She's going for the grassy area in front of the group of bungalows. Pull in behind her and stay in the vehicle." Steve released his gun strap. "Detective Tanner here. I'm on the corner of Ocean and Hemlock. Give me the backup's location? I can't wait five minutes to approach. I'm moving."

"Please, Steve, don't go alone. I got a nudge and knew something was coming, but your plan feels wrong." Page glanced at the sedan.

"I've got this." Steve reached for the door handle. "Stay put."

"I see two heads in the car. Last I checked, you have one, and it's not functioning so great." Page sighed as he closed the door and walked toward the jalopy.

Steve motioned for the driver to drop the window.

Another nudge, even stronger hit. Page knew what she must do. Grabbing the pistol from her purse, she tucked it into her pocket. Dropping down, she eased her way toward the passenger side of the jalopy and stopped a few feet behind it.

Steve gave a quick glance her way.

Page felt his wrath as she maneuvered to listen to the exchange.

"I'm Detective Tanner, and we've been looking to speak with you. Before I ask you to exit the vehicle and lean against the doors, do you have a weapon?"

"I'm not answering any questions or getting out of my car," Stella's country twang was gone and replaced by a Greek accent.

Steve bent down to see the other passenger. "What about you, Jewel? Judging by those suitcases, you two have travel plans. And, that information is according to your pal, Lucky."

The mystery of the other occupant was solved. "Just great. Jewel, the president of my fan club," Page murmured under her breath. She couldn't hear Jewel's reply, but the door remained closed. "Not good. He's going to shift gears into a tough guy."

"Ladies, I hate to see you acting uncooperative. I'd hoped we could spend a few minutes chatting about your friend, Dean. But hey, we can do this differently." Steve took his gun from the holster. "Let's try again. Both of you get out. Take it nice and slow. I want your hands on the hood of the car. You forced me to add the additional requirement. Now," demanded Steve.

Page watched the doors open and the women exit. She

received a nudge to act. Page grabbed her gun and moved closer to Jewel. Steve looked her way but remained focused on Stella and Jewel's actions. *Where was the squad car?*

Steve cuffed Stella. "It's special jewelry for you to wear." He pulled a pistol from her ankle strap. "I figured as much. Don't move an inch." Steve turned his attention to the other woman. "Come on, Jewel. You're next. Get over here, Stella, and put your hands on the hood."

In a flash, Jewel pivoted in the wrong direction and ran toward where Page waited. Acting lightning fast, Page's foot went out. Jewel cried out and fell face down into the grass. "Hello again."

"You," seethed Jewel, making a move to get up.

"Yep, and I'm still meddling. My gun is pointed your way, so I'd prefer it if you stayed face down." Page stepped back a few feet.

Steve came alongside. "I'd prefer you stay on the ground, too. I don't have another set of bracelets for you, Jewel."

"Dekara," Jewel cried out and pulled something from her arm.

Page chuckled. "I think she's got a personal problem. It could be she cozied up in a bed of sand spurs. Prickly beasts, aren't they, Jewel?"

Steve grinned and answered his cell phone. "I hear the officers coming now. Tell Koch I've got two additional guests needing accommodations."

The police cars pulled in, and two officers exited with guns drawn.

Steve signaled them to holster their weapons and approach. "Cuff this one. The other one's locked on the side mirror. They're uninvited visitors to our country. I'd like them to experience Shell Isle's police arresting protocol. Make sure you do this one by the book."

"Yes, sir." The officer cuffed Jewel and waited for her to stand.

Page noticed the sand spurs stuck to the woman's clothes, and two pressed into Jewel's cheek. "Nasty things. They can cause all manner of woes, but I suspect nothing compared to what awaits you." Page paused for effect. "Jewel, messing with me was your downfall, kako gynaika."

Jewel's eyes fired her last dagger to Page's back.

"I'll wait in the vehicle, Steve." Page saw Koch's unmarked SUV pull up.

He hurried past her but managed a few words. "Always in the thick of it, snoop."

"It's my gift!" Page hollered back. She waited a full ten minutes before Steve came to her.

"Don't get your hackles up, Sherlocka, but I'm riding with Koch to the station. I need to interrogate these Greek goddesses."

"But you're supposed to rest, and I need to feed us," Page reminded him.

"And I'm counting on it and giving you another lecture for not staying in the car."

"You needed my assistance, and you know it, buster. I'd like to come along and observe the interrogation."

"No can do. You've seen enough action tonight." Steve

touched the back of his head. "I can't engage you now. Drive my vehicle home. It's only a few blocks. You'll be safe. Give me an hour, and I'll have Koch drop me off at Hibiscus." Steve leaned inside and kissed Page fully on the lips. "See? I've got my wits about me." Steve walked toward the others.

"I may have lost mine," Page said, her heart in her mouth.

Steve jogged back. "I forgot. Two questions. Will you see to Barnacle? Second, I'm curious what were those Greek words you and Jewel spoke?

"I called Betsy a few minutes ago. Barn's fine. He's in the hammock snoozing. As for my rusty Greek, I hope I called her an evil woman." Page shrugged and gave a sheepish grin. "Oh, and Jewel said, 'Damn.'"

"What else do you speak, Sherlocka?" asked Steve, backing away, grinning.

"This and a lot of that. See ya soon."

Page drove to the cottage. She was surprised to see Andre's vehicle parked in the driveway. The officer was sitting in his SUV across the street. Page sent a wave his way.

"Finally!" exclaimed Betsy, standing in front of the stove. "I held supper for you and—" She craned her neck around the wall. "Where's Dreamboat? Is he okay?"

Andre hopped off the island's stool and came toward Page. "What about Steve?"

"He's fine. It's a mild concussion. I was three blocks from having him home when Stella and Jewel lost their invisible powers. Suffice it to say, they're on the way to the station. With any luck, Steve will show up here with some more pieces to our puzzle." Page hung her handbag on the hook and circled the stove, wearing a raised eyebrow in question.

"What's for our late supper?" Page lifted the foil covering a bowl and received a smack on her hand.

"Should we wait for Steve? I can keep things hot," offered Betsy.

The cuckoo came out, announcing eleven o'clock.

"Have I told you how much I hate that bird?" Betsy glared at the clock.

Page ignored the clock reference. "Steve would want us to eat. What can I do to help? Page tried to open the oven door.

"You and Andre sit in the dining room chairs. I'm serving." Betsy reached for a potholder and lifted the cast-iron skillet from the oven. "Ooh, smells heavenly. You're going to go bananas for this recipe."

"Bananas?" repeated Andre. "Could be a hint." He followed Page to the table.

The sound of the squeaky wheel announced the food trolley's arrival.

Barnacle hurried to the empty chair where his bowl waited.

"Two male suckers," mumbled Page to herself. "My, the trolley only appears when it's a new recipe. Ah, I see the dome food covers have been resurrected for a big ta-dah."

"Absolutely," said Betsy, taking her seat.

Page noted that Andre's expression looked both confused and worried. He probably recalled Webb's encounter with Betsy's Kicker Stew. "Enough suspense. What's going into my meal bowl?"

Betsy lifted the lid on a salad bowl. "We have a lovely Bets Mex Salad with black olives, romaine, chopped tomatillos, Carolina Reaper chili, avocado, of course, and a wine vinaigrette." Betsy's tongs filled three bowls.

"Wait, uno momento. Rewind to the Carolina Reaper chilies. That sounds worrisome to eat this late," said Page.

Andre stared at his bowl, denying his fork the chance to probe.

"Aren't they like the hottest chilies in the states?" Page moved pieces to the side of her bowl.

"No, the world, I think. It should provide quite the culinary experience. Dig in."

Page ate a few pieces of avocado and lettuce before employing her tried and true napkin disposal trick. Poor Andre was on his own. Page took the opportunity to distract Betsy by sharing the night's adventure, meeting Stella and Queen Jewel of the sand spurs.

"Couldn't happen to a nicer broad," said Betsy, taking the salad bowls to the kitchen.

Page sneaked two fresh napkins from the trolley and watched Andre pour his third glass of tea from the pitcher. "Sorry, I couldn't warn you."

He looked at her with tearing eyes as red as the Carolina Reapers he'd consumed and pointed to his throat.

"Can't talk, right? Been there more than once," said a sympathetic Page.

Betsy reappeared and lifted the dome. "Main entrée."

"Are there more grim reapers in this dish?" voiced a hoarse Andre.

Betsy looked askance. "I never repeat the same pepper at a meal. I employed my trusted jalapeño for this repast." She reached for the slotted serving spoon and Andre's empty bowl.

A starving Page held out hope. "Besides your friend the jalapeño, who else did you invite to our bowls?"

"I thawed out my tamale casserole with smoked gouda and raisins." Betsy passed a generous serving to Page. "It's a favorite of Page's. Bon appétit!"

Andre's face brightened. He spooned a hearty amount into his mouth, missing a warning glance from Page. The coughing commenced.

"Good gracious, you poor man, the duct tape must have affected your mouth's motor skills." Betsy leaned over and pounded Andre's back.

He pointed to the empty tea pitcher.

An understanding Page turned to Betsy. "Can you get more tea?" Somehow, she'd find a way to make the meal up to Andre.

Betsy scurried into the kitchen.

"Is there any hope for us with dessert, assuming I live?" Andre managed to whisper.

"Dessert is our best chance for something edible." Page patted his arm and disposed of most of her bowl's contents.

Page stopped Andre from giving his share to Barnacle. Betsy's French toast had come close to taking him out months ago. Instead, she carried their bowls to the kitchen. "All done.

Let me finish slicing the lemon for the tea while you eat."

"I think I'll save my calories for the special dessert I whipped up. You've got enough lemon. Drop the slices in, and we'll get right to the sweet."

Andre refilled his glass and gulped the contents. "I'm not sure about dessert. I'm pretty full after the two courses." He emptied another glass of liquid.

"So, besides bananas, what do you have in store for us?" Page stared at the last dome.

Betsy lifted the lid. "Betsy Goes Bananas."

"How bananas?" rasped an enlightened Andre.

"Banana sponge cake, banana simple syrup, banana and chocolate chips, and fresh banana slices. If you want, the banana ice cream is in the freezer." Betsy cut generous slices for everyone but missed the sighs of relief.

Page accepted the mega dose of sugar, knowing she'd need it to keep Steve awake. She was determined to fit more murder puzzle pieces that he'd surely bring later. Three suspects were encamped at Shell Isle's jail. Page felt a growing desperation for the inklings and nudges to direct her next movement in this confounding case.

CHAPTER 26

Long after Andre departed and Betsy declared herself "done in," Page heard a light tap at the door. A weary and too handsome face stared back. "Sorry it's so late, but I bring my pounding head and some good information if you'll feed me and tuck me in on Tilly's damn torture settee. By the way, I sent the officer home."

Page pulled Steve down to her level and touched her lips to his. "I'll feed you something not prepared by Betsy, then we'll talk. And when the cuckoo comes out at five o'clock, I'll tuck you in with an extra soft pillow."

"I'm putty in your hands. Another kiss would go a long way in helping me feel—"

"Food is what you need, Tanner. Come park yourself on the stool. I've kept your plate warm." Page reached for an oven mitt and pulled the dish from the oven. A slight smile flickered across Steve's face when she put the plate in front of him.

"Yep, a loaded hamburger with fries. Cop chow." Page popped the lid on a cola can." Here's your dose of caffeine.

"This burger looks great. It's even got grilled onions." Steve took a ginormous bite and bobbed his head, chewing. "Betsy's a fool commandeering the kitchen away from you."

"Don't I know it. You really missed out on tonight's

supper. The grim reaper visited our salads." Page rolled her eyes at Steve.

Steve tossed two fries into his mouth. "The grim reaper in a salad? Lay it on me. What did the fire starter serve?"

"Better to ask Andre. I fear he'll not come around here again."

"Duly noted. Let me finish my burger, and I'll fill you in on what little tonight's interrogation of Jewel and Stella produced."

"Of course, eat. How's your head feeling now?" Page moved around the island and touched the back of Steve's head. "Your egg laid an egg. It's bigger. I'm getting you an ice pack once you finish eating."

"I don't need —"

Page lifted an eyebrow.

"Thank you. An ice pack would be great," Steve's expression turned playful. "What would really be great is you snuggling with me on Tilly's —"

"For the millionth time, we'll have no hanky-panky under this roof." Betsy appeared wearing a grin and a tattered purple chenille robe. She poured a glass of water. "My Bets Mex Salad made me thirsty. How are you feeling, Dream... Steve?"

"Better, thanks." Steve placed the daisy cloth napkin next to his empty plate.

"Well, chickadees, back to bed for me. My lounger chair is heading to the beach in a few hours with or without an officer. Hurry and solve this case. You two behave. Nighty."

"Yes, Betsy," Page said, giving an indulgent laugh.

"I'll handle your protection tomorrow, princess. Tuck in." Steve winked at Page and moved to the sofa. He patted the cushion next to him. "Come hither, fair maiden."

Page grabbed an ice pack from the freezer. "I come bringing a gift, Prince Knows-a-Lot."

She handed him the cold bag. "Use it." Page sat next to him and reached for her notebook and pen. "Tell me what you got."

"Hey, this does help the pain." Steve adjusted the pack. "So, I'll start by saying the two women refused to cooperate. They knew we had nothing concrete to tie them to Dean other than your overhearing a vague but menacing conversation. They played dumb on being affiliated with Zeus Pharm. Basically, all they owned up to was being in the country illegally and using fake IDs."

"Geez, you already had that proof." Page laid the pen aside.

"Exactly."

"How about alibis for the night Dean was killed? I saw Stella and Lucky at the scene," reminded Page.

"Both maintained it was a pure coincidence they were there when Dean was killed. They'd planned a boat ride, which you saw them leave."

"Then, why come around and threaten me?" asked Page.

"Oh, Jewel had an answer waiting. She said they'd all been doing some shark fishing, which is against the law. She feared you'd turn them into the authorities, and they'd be caught as illegals. Pretty lame, I grant you." Steve shook the ice pack and repositioned it.

"Okay, so what's their reason for being in the country with fake IDs? This ought to be good." Page looked up and rolled her eyes.

"They wanted to come to the land of opportunity and not wait to live the dream. Jewel said the plan was to apply for citizenship at a later time. Oh, and Dean was their source for the fake identifications. We did confiscate two pistols from each that are heading to the ballistics lab."

"Great. More guns to muddy this case. So, let me see if I've got this ridiculous story right. Lucky, Jewel, and Stella traveled illegally to the land of opportunity. They took a boat out the night Dean was murdered for illegal fishing. Then, harassed me to keep quiet about said activity for fear of being arrested and discovered that they weren't welcome in our country. They knew Dean only as a source to get fake IDs. Yes?" Page gave a small, derisive laugh. "This is rich."

"It gets better." Steve handed Page the ice pack. "Thanks. When I asked why Lucky tried to kill Dean, the two women's rehearsed answers were priceless."

"Wait till I sit back down." Page returned the bag to the freezer. "Ready."

"Dean and Lucky had gotten into a scuffle over Stella. Both ladies threw Lucky under the bus and made it about jealousy. Stella claimed Lucky has an anger management problem. Supposedly, he went to the hospital to eliminate his competition. They held firm, Lucky was lying about them having any involvement in his dealings with Zeus and Dean. End of their story."

"Did you keep them overnight?"

"The sad truth is, we didn't have an isolated cell for women available. You know how small our station and jail are. Our DA didn't want to charge them until he talked to immigration this morning. He's learned the lesson on getting proper federal direction. We agreed to assign an officer to keep tabs on them. I explained to a worried Stella and Jewel that their next hours didn't include tonight's flight."

"At least we stopped them from fleeing." Page tapped her forehead, allowing the information to percolate. "Tell me there's a different officer on watch and not the one who let Tony slip away?"

"We're good. Koch insisted that he take the duty. After his part in their interrogation, Jewel and Stella's protests were priceless. They kept insisting on a woman. Koch ate that up."

"Did he do his big, bad intimidator act?" Page's eyes danced in merriment.

"Yep, the very one. His performance even made me nervous." Steve smiled at the thought.

Page sighed. "You still need ironclad proof to tie them to Lucky, Zeus, and Dean. Even if Lucky's gun killed Dean, they'll maintain ignorance. That's one fishy tale you caught and brought home. Pardon the pun."

"Yep, it stinks like yesterday's fish. Sorry. You started the fish repartee." Steve's lips moved into a smile. "Besides, it's the middle of the night, and we're both punchy."

"Maybe we are a little punchy." Page's head lifted to meet Steve's gaze. "Seriously, out of the three cases I've landed since moving to Shell Isle, this one is the most convoluted. It's starting to annoy the bejabbers out of me. Despite receiving inklings and nudges, I lack clarity around which of these dodgy suspects murdered Dean. And Betsy's right. We need to get this solved. We have Honey Bees buzzing, and I crave more sailing time on Carpe Diem."

"Hold on, first mate. What about Carpe's captain? Doesn't he rate—"

Page moved closer and buried her face into Steve's shoulder. "Oh, his rating will definitely improve if he helps me wrap up this murder. What's next?" Page moved to sit up.

"Stay close. I'll do a better job of answering." Steve's fingers wound through Page's hair. "It's like touching spun silk. He kissed the top of her head and then moved to capture her lips."

Page felt her heart do a flutter.

"Damn." Steve rubbed his forehead.

"See? You got too frisky." Page moved to the corner of the sofa.

"Betsy's cast some spell on us out here. I'm going to talk to her contractor and see if he can't hurry up with this renovation. She and the case are playing hell with our extracurriculars." Steve went to retrieve the ice pack.

Page gave a throaty laugh and noted how the ex-Seal exuded sex appeal just by opening a freezer door. She either needed her wits or Betsy's fan. Wits won out as Page watched him return to the sofa. "Better?"

"Depends on what better you're referring to? My head, some. My desire for—"

An amused Page covered his mouth with her hand.

"Enough. Focus. I repeat. What's your next move?"

"We're hoping to catch Tony and friend. He's top of the list now. My FBI buddy said Dean's father wanted Tony to bring his son to Chapel. Seems Tony's instructions were to find him, transport him, and/or silence him. It's the way these guys operate."

Page gulped. "As in silence Dean forever, amen?"

"Yes, ma'am. Remember, he'd been skimming from Mintto so he could disappear and start anew. It's why he fled and took on Dean Westin's identity. Another interesting piece is that Westin's government files have been corrupted. There's not a single bit of information on the man. It's been wiped. He doesn't exist."

"Meaning you can't trace back who on the inside helped Dean gain this person's identity? Talk about covering your tracks. Dean almost managed to achieve his new life, if not for Tony's gift of tracking down someone." Page gave a shiver.

"Bingo, Sherlocka." Steve pulled Page against him and stretched out on the sofa. He placed the ice pack in a nearby decorative glass bowl. "Can I please sleep now?"

"Not until the cuckoo—"

"I'm near cuckoo from exhaustion. Let's lay here together and relax…for a…."

Page glanced at Steve. Sleep had claimed him. The clock hands said he could rest. Head on his chest, Page drifted off listening to his steady heartbeat. Speeding cars and hit men chased her dreams.

CHAPTER 27

Page peered into her closet, wondering how to dress for the day. Thanks to Betsy's blabbering about the hellacious last twenty-four hours, Ina had insisted she take the day off, too. She felt confident that Ina and Daisy could handle Honey Bees. Still, she'd exacted a promise from Ina to ring them if they got busy.

For some odd reason, her hands put the jeans back on the shelf. Instead, Page opted for a printed cotton ruffled skirt and yellow peasant blouse. Wrapping an obi belt around her waist, the sleuth frowned at her image in the mirror. Why wasn't she dressed in her usual carefree beach attire? The inkling came in answer.

Page found Betsy staring absently into the pantry. An empty skillet waited on the cooktop, and empty it could stay. In a flash, she reached for a box of cereal. "What's up? Is Steve gone?"

Betsy pivoted, wearing an exasperated face. "What's up, you ask? For starters, I caught the pocket of my new orange-flowered Mumu on the door handle and ripped it a good three inches. I can't find any pimentos and capers to make our omelets. Barnacle is in the hammock waiting for chow. As for Detective Dreamboat, he rushed out of here after a call. He looked worse than a scruffy dog, too. Whiskers, wrinkled clothes, and more cowlicks than this guy, Jessup, I dated from Georgia—"

Page held up a hand. "Betsy, hold up. Can you tell me about Jessup and his cowlicks later? I got an inkling, and I need your help."

Betsy sighed and put the skillet back in the cabinet. "Just great. An inkling to start our day. Grab me a bowl, too. I hate cornflakes. Where are the bananas?"

Page pointed to the empty fruit basket. "You must have used them all for last night's dessert. I'll feed Barnacle while you get our cereal ready. Poor fellow carried his empty dish to his dining placemat." Page went to fill his bowl with kibble.

Betsy brought their cereal bowls to the table. The three ate a few bites in silence. "So, wanna tell me what this latest inkling has us doing?"

"I need to go to the high school," answered Page.

"Why the high school?" Betsy asked with a mouthful of cornflakes.

"I haven't a clue, but go, I must. The *how* is my problem. The officer is parked outside. It's not like I can hop in my SUV. You were always the one when we were teenagers who figured out ways to sneak out."

"With Lucky in the slammer and Stella and Jewel under watch, I don't think we need protection. Let's call Steve and tell him to set us free. I'm taking my lounger to the beach, come hell or high tide." Betsy moved Barnacle's dish closer to the table edge and gave him a pat.

"Let's not call Steve. Let's find a way for Page to sneak

out of Hibiscus and go on her mission. Then, you can spend the whole live long day on the beach with Dowager Margaret. Where are you going?" Page watched Betsy head toward the bedroom and reappear, holding her cell phone.

"Ina, we need a favor. Get Daisy situated at Honey Bees and swing by and pick up Page. She'll text you when and where. You're a doll." Betsy turned to Page. "Done. What else do you need?" She sat and put her spoon to work.

"What a brilliant move, Betsy Ross."

"I know. Now, how do you plan to leave? Want me to act as a decoy? I may have done a tiny bit of reconnoitering earlier. Our protector may be a tad overweight, but he's got the cutest baby face."

"Stop. I don't need a decoy. Here's the plan. I'll slip out the back of the cottage and walk to the beach-access parking lot. Ina can meet me there. I'll come back the same way." Page smiled reassuringly at Betsy.

"Good plan. I like it, but..." Betsy's mouth twisted.

"But what?"

"Don't you think I should come along?"

"Nope. You stay here in case Baby Face knocks on the door," explained Page.

"Ah, right. I'm your cover. Got it." Betsy bobbed her head. "And, when you get home, beach time for us. I'll even loan you one of my historical romances." Betsy carried the dishes to the sink.

Page ignored the novel offer. "Okay, I'm going to throw some lipstick and mascara on and text Ina. Is my phone—"

"Ringing? Yes, and my money is on Dreamboat missing

you and wanting to arrange...Page?" Betsy turned from the kitchen sink to see herself alone.

"Hey, Steve. How's the head?" asked Page, closing her bedroom door.

"Head's still sitting where it belongs. Listen, I've got news and hope you can intuit something to assist," said Steve.

"Shoot. Sorry. Tell me." Page applied a coral lipstick.

"We found the silver SUV."

"Super." She put the cell phone on speaker and pumped the mascara wand.

"Not super. We found Tony inside with a bullet to his head. The wise guy must have gotten orders to take him out since he was under our scrutiny. He'd become a liability like Dean."

"These people aren't nice. We've now lost our prime suspect. Any more happy news?" asked Page.

"Yeah, we confirmed Dean's real name. He was a junior Mintto. Get this. Senior said we could handle disposing of his son's body. He had no interest in having Junior return. What a low-life human being. Everything points to Mintto ordering both hits, but I can't prove it yet."

"I agree, on the surface it sure looks that way. Mintto is a slug." Page's lips twisted in disgust. "The reports on the guns are critical—"

"Speaking of guns, go figure this one. We got the results back on Jewel's pistol. The other three are hung up in processing. Her gun is clean," said Steve.

"Of course, her weapon passed. I never doubted it. Jewel's the one who calls the shot but doesn't deliver it."

"Another good pun, Sherlocka. Thanks for the bit of levity." Steve cleared his throat. "Here's another one for you. The officer watching the two women caught Stella trying to climb out of the motel room's bathroom window. Seems she found herself stuck mid-flight, so to say. He said something about her bra straps."

Page couldn't help but laugh, envisioning Stella's failed escape. "Now, that's hilarious."

"I thought so," Steve said with an indulgent laugh. "We brought Stella and Jewel back to the station. Also, we gave our three motleys another chance to sing, but not one carried a tune. Nothing more here."

"I appreciate your sharing and trust." Page snagged a tissue and blotted her lipstick.

"Hey, how about a tinkling for me?"

"A tinkling? Again, with this. You should be courting my good side, Detective Tanner. Calling my inklings… tinklings… just cost you."

"Ah, Sherlocka, give a guy recovering from a concussion a little break. You know I've grown to depend on your…inklings and those nudges, too. They're as spectacular as you. How am I doing? Better, right? You amazing sleuth."

Page heard the smile in Steve's voice. "Okay, you charmer, I promise to sing in tune when something of consequence comes to me. Tony may be gone, but he remains on our suspect board. I sense we're closer to solving this murder than we realize."

"From your mouth to the crime-busting gods' best ears." Steve's hand muffled the phone. "Hang on, Koch. Page,

I need to go. You and Betsy behave." Steve rang off before she had to answer.

Page knew the time wasn't right to tell Steve of the morning's inkling. She had her methods. Veering off a path that had served her for many years wasn't an option. She was going to the high school alone. Stealing one final glance in the mirror, Page texted loyal Ina instructions.

~*~

Wide sunglasses in place, Page made her escape down the beach toward the parking lot. She caught sight of Ina's car but had to wait for a group of excited kindergarteners to file past. Their teacher was engrossed in telling them about the jellyfish hunt. Page envied them the innocent world they inhabited.

"Hey, Ina. Boy, do I ever owe you for chauffeuring me to the high school." Page hopped in the front seat.

"It's no problem at all. Betsy called back and updated me on your sleuthing. Oy, if you gals don't land in mischief. I brought a box of our fresh baked cookies like you asked." Ina pointed to the back seat.

"Great. I don't think I'll need much time at the high school if you wouldn't mind waiting?" Page groaned when she realized part of her skirt was caught in the door.

"Not a problem, sista." Ina drove past the officer on duty. "Betsy's right. He's got a baby face." Ina half laughed.

"I should never have released Betsy from her no-man moratorium. She's managed to hang her cap on an officer —"

"Andre," finished Ina.

"I knew it. She's on the prowl." Page smiled through

narrow eyes. Their aqua color intensified. "Poor man. I'm not sure his digestive system will survive the onslaught."

Ina came to a stop sign and touched Page's arm. "I'm going to speak frankly. Are you planning to do anything remotely dangerous? I know your past, so don't go dodgy. I want the scoop."

"Truthfully, I'm not sure what I'm doing or who I'm seeing. I got an inkling this morning to go to the school. I guess you could say I'm flying by the seat of my britches." Page caught her bottom lip between her teeth.

"Knowing this, I'll keep the motor running and have the police station on speed dial." Ina accelerated.

"I don't think you'll see any action, but it's good to know my partner is at the ready. By the way, what kind of cookies?" asked an amused Page, observing Ina's death grip on the steering wheel.

"Peanut butter cup. I made sure not to grab Betsy's version," added Ina.

"Dare I ask?" Page waved to a young couple with a toddler crossing.

"Pumpkin peanut butter cup. What else?"

Page rolled her eyes at Ina. "My cousin is uncontrollable with a mixing bowl and spoon. Turn left at the first school entrance and park anywhere. Guess it's showtime."

Ina pulled in a slot in front of the main entrance. "Text me. Call me. For Pete's sake, be careful. Here, don't forget the box to sweeten up someone."

"Got it. Back soon without guns a-blazing. I promise." Within seconds of entering the school, Page got her nudge.

She headed to the office with her request.

CHAPTER 28

Principal Holly rounded the corner as Page reached for the main office door. "Hello again. It's Page?" His smile seemed geared toward parents. One that never quite found his eyes but meant to appear friendly.

"Hello, and yes, good memory. I'm Page Wright, co-owner of Honey Bees and consultant for the police department. At the moment, I'm wearing a consultant hat. I was going into the office to see if I might arrange a few minutes to speak with the computer science teacher."

Holly crossed his arms. "I see. Are you able to share the reason for this request?"

Page sensed she'd better give him something plausible if she wanted to get past the roadblock. "First, I brought her some cookies, and second, I need to ask—what's her name again?"

"It's Mary Sue Wheeler. What type of questions, if you don't mind me asking?" The smile abandoned the man's face.

"I don't mind your asking at all, but they're of a highly personal nature. As a consultant, the detectives felt a female is more appropriate to ask these types of questions." Page paused to take a read on Holly. He wasn't sold.

"I'm not sure it would be in Ms. Wheeler's best interest—"

"I can certainly understand your feelings. That's why I chose to come myself. I feared bringing Ms. Wheeler into the station for questioning might cue the reporters parked outside the department's door. They're always looking for any story to splash on the front page of the *Shell Isle Trumpet*." Page's last salvo hit its mark.

Holly's face turned ashen. "I think you've painted a clear picture. Such publicity isn't what my school needs. Please follow me." The principal's hand indicated the direction.

"Thank you." Page kept her expression friendly.

"I'll take you to Mary Sue's classroom myself. May I have your assurance that you will keep this visit low-key?"

"Of course." Page waited while he tapped on the door.

"Ms. Wheeler, do you have a class?" asked Principal Holly.

Mary Sue popped her head out of her door and looked at Page, puzzled. "Not for another twenty minutes. Why?"

"This is Page —?" Holly stopped.

"Wright. Hi, Mary Sue. I'm Page Wright, a consultant for the Shell Isle Police Department. I'd like a few minutes of your time."

"Why do the police want to talk to me?" Panic sounded in Mary Sue's voice.

"You're in absolutely no trouble at all. I'd appreciate getting your thoughts on someone you know." Page turned to Holly. "We're good here. Thanks again for your cooperation."

"If you both need me —"

"Thank you, Principal Holly. Drop by Honey Bees soon. I'd like to get your opinion on our popular peanut butter cup cookies. Fact is, I brought a box to Mary Sue."

The teacher smiled and accepted the box. "How lovely of you. I adore Honey Bees. Everyone does. Oh, yes, now I know you; you're one of the owners."

Page turned her back dismissively to Holly. "We love compliments. Mary Sue, may I come inside your classroom? Feel free to try one of those cookies now."

Holly mumbled something and retreated.

Mary Sue opened the class door. Page chose a computer station closest to the teacher's desk and sat. Surprised, she watched Mary Sue pull a chair close to her and open the box of cookies.

"These look yummy. I'm going to indulge myself with one. What do you want to ask me?"

Page dove in. "I'd like to ask you about Dean Westin, the deceased math teacher who taught down the hall. Can you tell me what you thought of him?"

"As a teacher?" Mary Sue broke off a piece of the cookie and chewed.

"As a man." Page probed.

Mary Sue coughed. "As a man? Well, honestly, I wouldn't know him in such a way—"

Page softened her expression. "Look, I'm going to speak frankly. We're trying to figure out if Dean had any outside involvement with corporate espionage. You could, without being aware, have inside knowledge of what Dean could have been doing. Did you notice anything that seemed out of character for a high school math teacher?"

Mary Sue swallowed. "Actually, I might know a little

something, but I'd appreciate it if you didn't tell Principal Holly what I told you. I wouldn't want to lose my job. He doesn't abide gossiping."

Page raised her right hand. "Not a word from me to Holly. Please tell me."

Mary Sue leaned closer. "Here's what I saw and heard last week."

~*~

Page ran to Ina's car. Breathless, she climbed inside. "Get me back to the beach parking lot."

"You got the goods, didn't you? I knew you would." Ina put the vehicle in gear.

"Yep, I think I've got something which finally makes sense. We'll know soon enough." Page glanced at her phone, relieved to see no missed calls. As Ina drove, a plan began to form in her mind, powered by a nudge growing stronger. Ina's voice brought her back.

"I won't ask for details because I respect how you like to sleuth around. Still, you need to act cautiously." Ina pulled into the beach access lot and handed Page a small sack. "For you. Something you love and seldom get to enjoy."

"What?" Page peeked in the bag. "A knish. It smells divine." Page wrapped the napkin around the fried treat. "Ina, I adore you and this potato knish. Did you make it?"

Ina nodded, wearing a pleased expression. "I adore you and Betsy right back. Now, go sneak back into Hibiscus and get this murderer behind bars. You two are needed at Honey Bees post haste."

~*~

"Where are you, Betsy?" Page, closing the sliding door, noticed Barnacle chewing on a soup bone and back in the hammock. "Betsy?"

"I'm right here. I was in the den sewing my Mumu, wondering when we could beach it." Betsy halted. Her mouth thinned. "I know that look."

"Get our recipe. Time to bake the cake." Page pulled out the mixing bowls.

Betsy's eyes grew wide. "Hold the fort, General. Are you telling me we're baking — ?"

"Yep, we're delivering an enchanted honey cake to our murderer. Shake a leg. Don't you want to spend the afternoon ogling the lifeguard?"

"You know me too well." Betsy reached for the special honey. "I expect you to fill me in on the details while we make our cake. You may keep Detective Dreamboat out of the loop, but never Betsy Ross, possible ancestor to the sewer of —"

"Our flag," finished Page. "I've got the teaspoon. Hand me the secret spice jar. You mix while I talk. It's quite a twisted tale."

CHAPTER 29

"This is the most delectable honey cake we've made yet. It's so golden and smells like ambrosia." Betsy tasted a crumb. "Mmm. What's got you lost in the phone screen?"

"Oh, this is providence. Steve just texted me that he's pulled the officer off watch here and will explain soon." Page peeked out the kitchen window. "Yep, he's gone. Let's go, Bets. Operation Bee Sting awaits."

"I'm driving. You hold the cake." Betsy grabbed her keys and pointed toward the door. Her face was flushed. "This rushing to bake the honey cake has rewarded me with a hot flash to beat the band."

"You can turn the AC on high and turn all the vents your way." Page followed her cousin, bringing trepidations. Betsy's love affair with pumping the gas pedal and braking with vigor always promised Page a queasy tummy. She needed to be firing on all cylinders. Page dropped her sunglasses, approaching Betsy's car. "Your bright yellow buggy is going to announce our arrival a block away. Maybe I should drive—?"

"Stop dissing my wheels and get in. I always drive to the honey cake's destination. It gives you time to mentally prepare and get more insights." Betsy cranked the engine and aimed every air vent full blast her way. "Better. Are we ready to do this?"

"Yep." Page fist-bumped Betsy. "These two Honey Bees are about to sting an unsuspecting murderer. Drive on."

"That's the spirit. Let's go over the plan one more time." Betsy's foot went to work on the car's pedals.

Page popped a peppermint, anticipating her stomach's reaction. "Okay, you're to call Steve once we arrive. As luck would have it, the police station is two blocks away from our destination, so he can get to us fast. I'll make sure the door is unlocked so he can listen. Same as the other times. Easy."

"Except I'm outside doing all the worrying about you on the inside. And lest you forget, it's me who endures Detective Dreamboat's wrath when I make the call. It's all most unpleasant." Betsy lamented.

"Dear oh dear, how you suffer while I'm having a friendly visit with a murderer. Yep, you definitely drew the short straw in our sleuthing roles," teased Page. Her cell phone rang.

"Who's calling?" asked Betsy.

"Dreamboat, who else? Hi Steve. What's up?" Page put the phone on speaker and laid it in the console. She signaled Betsy to stay silent.

"As promised, I'm back and bringing good news. All of the ballistic reports are in front of me. We know who-dun-it."

"You do? Awesome. Do I have to guess?" asked Page.

"You could, but you'd be wrong. It's Stella."

"Stella?" repeated Page. Her brows knitted together. "You're sure?"

"Yes, ma'am. The gun has her and Dean's fingerprints. The bullets were a perfect match. Maybe she and Dean had a lovers' tiff or something along those lines. It's an all-too-common motive."

"Possibly so. What's your plan of action?" Page tried to keep her voice steady.

"Once we talk to the district attorney, we'll do more questioning and then charge her. We need to dot all the *i*'s because she's not a citizen."

Page's mind scrambled for the best reply. "Well, it sounds like you've got this case sorted."

"What a tough case it has been, too. Still, we've locked it up in a matter of days. Want to celebrate tonight? Let's take Carpe Diem out for a sail."

"I'd love to get out on the water. Let's chat more later." Page pointed for Betsy to turn right. She tossed the cell phone in her handbag. Page released a long exhale and glanced at Betsy.

"That was certainly unexpected." Betsy's expression changed to worry.

"Yes and no," answered Page cryptically. A fresh inkling came. A smile lit up her face.

"Change of plans?" asked a confused Betsy.

"Nope. There's the place up ahead. Turn in." Page waited for Betsy to park. "Okay, I'm calling your phone now. You'll be able to listen. Here's the other phone to ring, Steve."

Betsy nodded. "Promise me you'll take care and stay on script?"

Page grinned. "Piece of cake." She held up the honey

cake. "Call Steve once you see me go inside. It's time this bee stings an unsuspecting someone."

The brick ranch home was nondescript. The yard showed minimal care as Page approached the front door. Stealing a breath, she knocked and put her smile in place.

"Yes? Oh, it's you. The Honey Bees lady."

"Yep, Mr. Park, it's me. I'm delivering you a special gift and message from Mary Sue. May I come in for just a minute?" Page marched past the surprised face.

"Excuse me, but I'm sort of busy. I took the day off. My wife is away at some fancy spa for a week." Amos Park followed Page into the kitchen.

She saw his surprise was replaced by annoyance. "I understand, but Mary Sue is such a sweetie, you must allow me to do as she asked." Page made her smile bigger. "First, she asked that I tell you she's looking forward to the swim. She's coming over in an hour. Between you and me, I think she's quite smitten by you."

"I have that effect on most women. How about you? Like what you see? I dig older chicks who keep themselves fit." Amos moved closer to Page.

She had to adjust her plan or risk losing the opportunity. "Thanks, I'm flattered, but Mary Sue and I are friends. I can't tread on her territory. Anyway, she asked me to bake this special Old World honey cake and bring it to you. I hear you have quite the sweet tooth, Amos." Page reached for a plate, knife, and fork in the dish rack.

"Yeah, I like good desserts. What are you doing now? Just leave the damn cake and take off."

Page ignored him. "Oh, I almost forgot. Mary Sue's bringing the ice cream." Page cut a slice. "Here you go, Amos. Before I leave, I'm anxious to know if you will take to this special recipe. Give a taste for me...please." Page made her lips pout and batted her lashes.

"You're a little minx. Aren't you?" Amos put a generous bite in his mouth and then another.

"Well? Have I ignited your passion for my honey cake?" Page turned up her flirt and trusted the inkling would bring a sweet reward.

Amos glanced at her chewing and forked another chunk. "I've never tasted anything like this before. I feel all mellow like —"

"I told you the cake is special. It's the honey and spice blend. Here. Let me cut another slice for you." Page placed a huge piece on Amos's empty plate. "Hey, I heard something interesting about Dean Westin's case. You might want to hear it since you both taught together. Page set her first hook.

"What news?" Amos continued to eat.

"Dean died. They're arresting someone named Stella for the murder. I heard her gun was tied to the bullet pulled from poor Dean. Seems he and Stella were involved in corporate espionage and tied to a group from an island off Greece. I understand Dean was the math brain, decoding ciphers and formulas."

"Is that a fact?" Amos looked mildly interested.

"I can't imagine being so smart as to know how to unravel complicated formulas. It's a real turn-on." Page felt a shiver run through her body. She had to continue the act to draw Amos out. Judging by his eyes, the honey cake's magic had kicked in. Time was of the essence.

"Dean wasn't smart. He was an idiot."

"I agree. I bet you had to help dumb Dean break the code. Didn't you, Amos? All those complicated formulas I saw on your chalkboard were smart. And you had Mary Sue helping with the tech part. You were the brains behind the scheme, but you didn't get credit." Page shook her head in mock disgust.

"Like I said, Dean was an idiot."

"Wanna hear my theory on how Dean met his end?" Page cut Amos another slice of cake. "I'm a sleuth and, like you, I love puzzles. This one was challenging because I was up against your keen intellect."

"Yeah, now I remember you coming to the school with that detective. Let me hear your theory. We'll see how smart you really are." Amos grabbed a carton from the refrigerator and poured a glass of milk.

"Okay. Correct me when I'm wrong. Like I said, Dean had this corporate gig tied with Stella and the rest. He was a simple accountant and not a math whiz like you. Dean got in over his head and couldn't deliver the formulas, so he wisely came to you. You agreed to help him, and he probably paid you a pittance. How am I doing so far?"

"I don't know why I'm playing along. You're treading in deep waters." Amos rubbed his forehead. "I don't feel myself at all." His expression softened.

"It's the cake's gift to you. Enjoy it while it lasts. So, to continue, you rightfully got fed up with the arrangement. You confronted Dean. I suspect he pulled a gun, and you tussled. What I can't figure out is why Dean had Stella's pistol?"

"Easy. She loaned it to Dean for the rendezvous with the lab rat. That guy is unhinged," blurted Amos.

"Ah, makes sense. Murder by the numbers. Dean was accidentally shot. You immediately saw the opportunity to take over the work and make some nice jingle. I think you found Stella, Jewel, and Lucky and told them you'd shot Dean dead. You cleverly made them an offer they couldn't refuse. Jewel, being the leader, went for it. She paid you to handle the number ciphering and the last exchange."

"You tell a good story, but you're off track. Jewel isn't the leader. Is that as far as you've got?"

"No. You take the meeting at the Crab Shak and do the exchange in the men's room. Only someone in there overhears you and the lab rat from LRN Labs." Page forced a laugh. "I gotta hand it to you. I've never seen a cop strapped to a toilet, dressed in duct tape and bungee cords. It was hilarious and again well executed by you, no doubt."

Amos's mouth jerked into a grin. He said nothing.

Page knew she needed to wrap things before the honey cake's powers ebbed. She took a risk and touched Amos's arm. "Here's another thing I can't figure out. Help me, please." Who did Stella meet in the Crab Shak's parking lot and why? It couldn't have been you. The lab rat had just passed you the laptop, so you hadn't time to decode it. I'm baffled."

"Maybe I had something Stella wanted." An evil look came into Amos's eyes.

Page got the insight. "Stella wanted her gun back, and

you had it. Yes, now I see."

"Listen. I'm getting bored. It's time we end your puzzle-solving game." Amos moved closer to Page.

"Hang on a sec. Don't leave a girl wanting. Stella's going down for Dean's death because you wiped your prints off the gun. I bet you made sure Dean's prints were on it. Brilliant, Amos. It's an open and shut case as far as the police are concerned. You've got a nice chunk of money for a little effort, and that suitcase waiting in the corner is taking you away. You're not waiting on Mary Sue." Page's lips trembled around her words. She feared she'd gone too far. Relief washed over her as she caught sight of Steve's angry face signaling her behind the foyer wall.

"I've heard enough out of you. Now, I've got a new problem to remedy, and I'm staring at it." Amos grabbed for Page, but she moved faster. "Ah, you want to play coy."

"Coy is me. Why don't I leave, and we'll forget all about our chat? You can keep the cake," offered Page, trying to put more space between them.

"I've got a better idea. You and I will take a little ride out by the jetty. It's shark feeding time." Amos advanced, grabbing for Page.

"Amos Park, don't move another inch. You're under arrest. Page, get to the foyer." Steve shoved Amos down on the counter.

Andre appeared and put the handcuffs on Amos. "We meet again. Only this time, I get the pleasure of dressing you in Shell Isle Police jewelry. I might throw in some duct tape later."

Amos tried to jerk away. "This is entrapment. You can't arrest me!" he yelled through clenched teeth. "She drugged me with that cake. I didn't know what I was saying."

Steve took over and marched Amos toward the door where Koch waited. "Try to convince any jury that a cake caused you to confess a lie. That might get you some time in a mental facility. I hear they're worse than prison if you're half sane."

"That woman is a witch or something!" wailed Amos. "I'm not crazy. She makes you act crazy. You guys need to listen to me."

"Shut up and get inside the car. We'll treat you to a nice psych evaluation during your stay with us." Koch shut the vehicle door and winked at Page.

Andre and Steve stood on each side of Page, watching the SUV haul Amos away.

Page sighed. "That was not my favorite takedown. Where's Betsy?"

Andre chuckled. "I had to get an officer to restrain her in that yellow banana she drives. She was hell-bent on coming to save you. I'll walk you out."

Steve reached for Page's arm. "Hang on there, Sherlocka. You've got me to deal with before Betsy."

"I'll pass." Page gave her detective a saucy look. "This is where I get lectured on my methods, and you threaten—"

Steve pulled Page into him and sealed her mouth with a kiss.

"Hey, I might grow to like this new type of lecture. What else do you have to say, Tanner?" Page waited breathlessly for his reply.

Plenty." Steve wrapped his arms around Page's waist and did an encore.

Betsy appeared. "Jeez, Louise. Is there any place you two won't do hanky-panky? Come on, Andre. You still owe me lunch at the Crab Shak. Let's leave these two to their hormones."

Steve grinned down at Page. "After we file the reports, how about we seize the day?"

Page nodded. "Carpe Diem, we're on our way."

ABOUT THE AUTHOR

As an author, Tonya's moved by the effect humor and narratives have on readers. That observation illuminates why her stories often convey messages inviting personal exploration. She is enthusiastic about crafting stories with beguiling characters, adding dashes of snappy humor, and engaging dialogue that leaves her fingerprint on each page.

When Tonya relocated to the mountains, she found fresh writing ideas waiting. From her favorite porch chair, gazing at a tranquil lake, the nudge to scribe her first novel came calling. From her beach chair, she got the idea for a cozy series, Shell Isle Mysteries. Tonya confesses to a new respect for a chair's ability to motivate her. She chases her writing joy from the mountains to the seashore.

TONYA PENROSE AVAILABLE BOOKS:

SHELL ISLE MYSTERY SERIES
World Castle Publishing
Baubles to Die For
Red, White, and Boom
Murder by Numbers

The characters of Page and Betsy keep chattering to Tonya, so expect future stories in this collection.

OTHER BOOKS by Tonya Penrose

Welcome to Charm
A Secret Gift
Old Mountain Cassie: The Three Lessons
Venetian Rhapsody

Tonya's fiction and non-fiction stories are published in numerous anthologies, e-magazines, local press, and literary magazines. Find Tonya listed in the Poets and Writers Directory.

Please consider this your invitation to visit:www.tonyawrites.com
Twitter @TonyaWrites

If you enjoy Tonya Penrose's (pen name) novels, please tell others, and take a moment to leave reviews.

BETSY'S RECIPES

Betsy's Hotsy Totsy Chips*
9 unpeeled medium white potatoes
4-5 teaspoons sea salt
2 teaspoons garlic powder
1 teaspoon cayenne
1 teaspoon white pepper
1 teaspoon black pepper
1 teaspoon marjoram
1 tablespoon chives
2.5 quarts ice water
A jar of imported honey mustard
Jalapeños minced

Wash the potatoes. Slice them very, very thin. Place the potatoes in the ice bath for 30-40 minutes. While they're bathing, mix all the dry spices in a small bowl.
Drain the potatoes and pat dry with paper towels.
In a heavy skillet, heat peanut oil until hot. Add the potatoes and stir often until crispy golden. Remove to a platter lined with paper towels. Let drain. Sprinkle seasoning over chips and toss. Place on a platter with dipping sauce in the center. Serve immediately. Get ready for compliments.
Empty the jar of honey mustard in a lovely ceramic dish and stir in the minced jalapeños. Cover and set aside until dipping time.

Serves 4 nicely
Omit Betsy's recipe changes: marjoram, chives, and all peppers except black. The dipping sauce is a personal preference.

Betsy's Breakfast Pep in Your Step*
2.5 pounds grated purple potatoes or 2 pounds frozen hash browns (thawed)
1/2 cup crumbled bleu cheese
1 cup shredded mild Cheddar cheese
8 oz. organic sour cream from contented cows
1/3 cup melted organic butter
2/3 cup chopped Vidalia onions
1 can cream of chicken soup
1/2 teaspoon salt
Fresh ground black pepper. Don't be stingy
1 cup cooked crumbled bacon
2 tablespoons of capers
1/2 cup chopped jalapenos
1 T Betsy's secret herbs (parsley, paprika, garlic powder)

In a colorful bowl to lift your spirits, combine hashers, soup, butter, cheeses, sour cream, onions, salt, lots of pepper, spices, herbs, capers, jalapenos. Mix gently and pour into an oiled glass 9x13 baking dish. Sprinkle bacon on top.
Bake at 350 until bubbly and hot.
Serve with popovers and a flavorful honey from Honey Bees. (You can find Ina's popover recipe in the book *Red, White, and Boom.*)

Serves 6
Omit Betsy's recipe changes: purple potatoes, jalapenos, bleu cheese, capers, and herbs.

Betsy's Rarin' Rhubarb Cream Pie*
1 (9-inch-deep pie crust) Don't fuss making your own.
1/4 cup organic white flour
3/4 teaspoon nutmeg
3/4 teaspoon cardamon
1 1/2 cups organic white sugar
3-4 cups chopped fresh rhubarb
3 large organic beaten eggs from happy hens
1 jar butterscotch sauce
1/2 organic sliced strawberries (Don't you dare buy frozen.)

Preheat the oven to 400 degrees.
In a large glass bowl, combine dry ingredients. Add beaten eggs. Toss in the chopped rhubarb and stir. Pour into the pie crust. Bake for an hour more or less.
Before serving, drizzle warm butterscotch sauce over the slice and garnish with strawberries. My added touch makes this pie yum.
Serves 6-8
Omit Betsy's recipe changes: cardamon and butterscotch sauce.

Betsy's Grim Reaper Mex Salad*
4 cups washed and torn romaine lettuce

1 large seedless English cucumber sliced
3 green onions chopped
4 organic Roma tomatoes chopped
1/2 cup chopped cilantro
2-3 grim reaper peppers minced
1/2 cup fresh corn kernels
1/4 canned black beans rinsed
3 sliced avocados bathed in lime juice
Salt to taste
Freshly ground black pepper
Crumbled tortilla chips

Place lettuce, cucumbers, tomatoes, cilantro, green onions in a festive salad bowl. Top with corn, beans, and avocados. Add salt, pepper, and the reapers.
Bring to the table and make a big ta dah for your guests before tossing with red wine vinegar and olive oil.
Top with chips.
Serves 4
Omit Betsy's recipe change: grim reaper peppers

Betsy Goes Bananas*
1/2 cup organic butter softened
1 cup flour
2 ripe bananas mashed
3/4 cup organic white sugar
2 large organic eggs from happy hens
1 teaspoon baking powder

1 teaspoon baking soda
2-3 tablespoons organic milk
1 teaspoon banana extract
1/2 cup semi-sweet chocolate chips
1/2 cup chopped pecans
Banana ice cream

Preheat oven to 350 degrees
Line two cake pans with wax or parchment paper and then grease with oil.
In a bowl, mix sugar and butter until smooth. Add mashed bananas, extract, and the eggs one at a time. Warm the milk in the microwave for 20-30 seconds. Add to the mixture and stir gently. Next add the baking soda. Sift the baking powder and flour so it's not crumbly. Fold into the mixture. Pour half the mixture in each cake pan.
Bake for 20-25 minutes until toothpick comes out clean. Sprinkle each cake with semi-sweet chocolate chips and allow to melt. When ready to serve, top with sliced bananas and pecans. Offer banana ice cream to the ones with a big, sweet tooth.
Omit from Betsy's recipe: Nothing. Yep, you read it right. Her addition of chips, pecans, bananas, and ice cream received Ina's blessing.

Betsy's Enchanted Honey Cake*
3 2/3 cups all-purpose flour

1 teaspoon baking soda
teaspoon Celtic salt
1 tablespoon baking powder
1 cup quality vegetable oil
1 cup of the honey bees' magical nectar
1 1/2 cups organic sugar
1/2 cup dark brown sugar
3 large organic eggs from happy hens
½ cup orange juice
2-3 tablespoons Kentucky Bourbon (optional)
3/4 teaspoon vanilla extract (Don't dare use imitation extract.)
1 cup coffee freshly brewed (I prefer a dark French roast.)

Set the oven at 345 degrees. (I find most ovens run hot.) Spray a 9x13 pan liberally with butter-flavored baking spray. (Page likes a Bundt pan, but I don't. Too finicky to get my cake out.) In a rainbow-colored ceramic bowl (No eyebrow-raising. You are making magic here.), mix the flour, salt, soda, and powder. In a separate bowl, combine the oil, ¾ cup of the honey nectar, sugars, eggs, coffee, vanilla, and juice. Mix. Add the wet mixture to the dry until everyone looks married nicely.
 Pour the magic into the pan. Drizzle the remaining nectar atop the batter in a lovely pattern. Bake until done. I start testing with a toothpick after 30 minutes. Let the enchanted honey cake cool before removing it from the pan. I drizzle more nectar on top, but that's just me helping Page solve our latest caper.
* Betsy agreed to share the basic honey cake recipe but confessed what makes her cake enchanted is the special kind of honey. That's

her secret, and she won't divulge the source of this amazing nectar. It seems our Betsy can keep her yap shut when it comes to creating magic for garnering a confession and closing a murder case.